THE SIREN SERIES

SiRen's Call

USA TODAY BESTSELLING AUTHOR
JESSICA CAGE

1

Written by Jessica Cage

Edited by Debbi Watson

Additional Editing by Joseph Editorial Services

Cover Design by: Solidarity Graphics

ISBN-13: **978-1-7364885-3-9**

AUTOGRAPH PAGE

Beware the call of the Siren!

Take

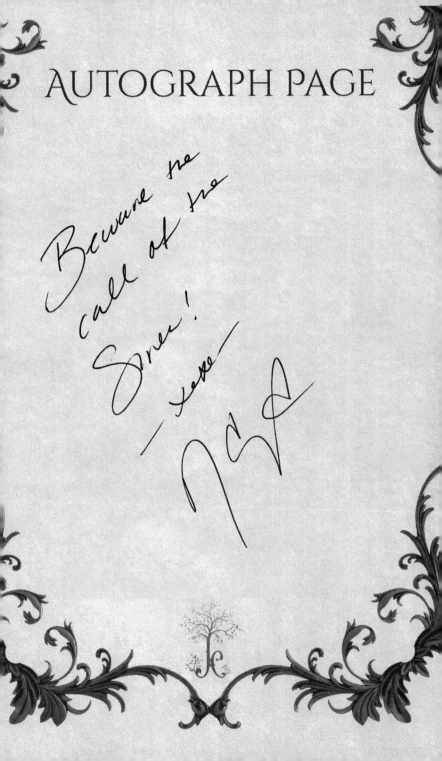

Contents

Dedication   VII

Acknowledgments   VIII

TRIGGER WARNING   IX

1. CHAPTER 1   1

2. CHAPTER 2   13

3. CHAPTER 3   25

4. CHAPTER 4   35

5. CHAPTER 5   45

6. CHAPTER 6   63

7. CHAPTER 7   77

8. CHAPTER 8   89

9.   CHAPTER 9   105

10. CHAPTER 10   119

11. CHAPTER 11   137

12. CHAPTER 12   153

13. CHAPTER 13   167

14. CHAPTER 14   181

15. CHAPTER 15   197

16. CHAPTER 16   205

17. CHAPTER 17   221

18. CHAPTER 18   233

19. CHAPTER 19   245

20. CHAPTER 20   261

21. CHAPTER 21   271

22. CHAPTER 22   285

23. CHAPTER 23   297

A dive into book2...   309

SIREN'S TEST   313

About the Author   319

DEDICATION

To you
Who believe
In the mythical
Magical
Worlds we weave.

ACKNOWLEDGMENTS

Special thanks to a special man. You lent me your ear and your knowledge of Greek Mythology and asked for nothing in return. Though you requested no acknowledgment, it would go against what I stand for if I didn't say thank you. Your encouragement and support are greatly appreciated. You may remain in the shadows...

To my Beta readers, you ladies are awesome, and your response to this story made it more enjoyable for me to write. I can never thank you enough for your honesty and enthusiasm.

TRIGGER WARNING

Hello Reader,
After listening to my reader feedback, I've updated the copies to include this Trigger Warning. The first chapters speak about SA, and there is a scene that has some uncomfortable details.

Because of this, I've added a stop page. Continue reading until you see the Black Warning page that tells you which page to skip to.

We all love fantasy, and I want this to be a safe space for all my readers.

Happy Reading
~Jessica

CHAPTER I

*W*hen it happened, I couldn't have been more terrified,
or more grateful.

My internship had run late, leaving me walking home from
my train on a bitterly cold, pitch-black night. The weather app
on my phone reported it was only ten degrees! If you referred to
my chattering bones, however, it was more like twenty below.

Winter was settling, securing its icy grip on Chicago, and
because ego made me bold enough to believe I could make it
home before sundown, my attire did little to protect me from
the hawk. I still had my bear, a tan fur and leather reversible coat
my aunt had given me, packed up far in the back of my closet. I
made a mental note to dig it out as soon as I got home.

1

Seven buildings away from my home, a rusted car flew by me. It was impossible to tell the make or model of the beat-up sedan because it looked as if they had ripped each piece of metal that covered it from a different unwilling donor, a junkyard makeover. They may have continued their way had I not lifted my eyes from my phone.

Through the dark driver-side window, I met two dark eyes, and my stomach lurched. I counted the shadows within. There were five men packed in the car, and the driver had his eyes on me. I averted my eyes. Now just five buildings between me and my own, the steps that led up to the front door of my apartment were within view. I was so close to safety that I quickened my pace.

The foolish hope that had filled my heart, the thought I would make it home unharmed, snapped with the squealing of worn brakes. The car slowed just enough to make a U-turn at the end of the block before making the slow creep back toward me, and my heart raced.

I scanned the streets for any signs of life. It was only 9:30, but with the drop in the temperature, there weren't too many people eager to hang around outside. There was no one to call. No one to witness what I knew was about to happen. Numb fingers fumbled with my phone. I could call the police. They wouldn't make it to me in time, but at least someone would know, and perhaps help would be on the way.

My hands trembled as I tried to unlock the screen and watch as the car neared at the same time. My nerves caused me to lose my grip, and as I watched my phone fall, I knew there was no time to recover it. Before it hit the ground, the car doors opened, followed by drunken catcalls and heavy footsteps. I froze.

"Hey, mama. Just stay right there, baby. I'm coming for you," the driver called to me as he slammed his door. His passengers, four of them, flocked behind him on either side, whistling and making noises that made my skin crawl. I tried to move, tried to force my legs to run, but they surrounded me before my brain processed what was happening.

I clutched my purse, but they weren't interested in my soon-to-be expired bus pass and scribbled work notes. This was not a mugging in the making; it was something so much more, so much worse.

"Please, leave me alone." My voice was low and trembling with fear, but they heard me. I could tell by the murmurs and low laughter that echoed in the surrounding air. My plea was nothing more than a tease to them.

"Leave you alone? Weren't you out here waiting for me, baby? I saw you. You want me, don't you, baby?" He was taller than I was. Staring straight ahead, I could see his lips, full and pink with red slits, caused by the chill in the air, or by underlining disease. His teeth were yellow and crooked, and his breath was a mixture of onions and liquor, something hard. It burned my nostrils.

"I just want to go home," I admitted, though it wouldn't make any difference. He wouldn't allow my freedom before he did whatever it was he planned to do.

"Oh, you will, just as soon as I am done with you." He confirmed my thoughts as he flicked the hood off my head. "Damn, baby. You are gorgeous." He looked at his pals for confirmation as he grabbed a handful of my hair that spilled out of my hood and down my shoulders. "Isn't she beautiful, fellas?" He wrapped his hand in my hair and yanked it, turning me around to see his friends.

They were bottom feeders. "The people of the night," as my aunt Noreen referred to them. They lurked the streets, waiting for someone to harass while partaking in their addiction of choice, drugs or drinking. This crowd looked as though they enjoyed both. The glazed-over look in the eyes of an alcoholic and the fidgety movements of a crackhead. The closer they got to me, the more I wanted to run, but I choked on my own panic.

"Please don't," I managed a broken whisper. It was useless to beg for my life, but I had to try.

"Shh." He leaned into me, his rancid breath creeping across my skin and making my stomach seize. "You are going to enjoy this, baby."

His hand reached out to me, and he unzipped my jacket. The cold air assaulted me. I tried to focus on the numbing effect it had and not his hand, which had found its way inside my shirt. He rubbed the outside of my bra and kissed my cheek. "Mmm, baby, you feel good." He looked at his friends who hovered, waiting for direction. "I think I want this one for myself, boys."

Disappointment stretched across each of their faces, echoed by groans of exasperation. Then there was pain. A sharp prick at the side of my neck. I looked down to see what it was and watched in horror as his hand pulled away from me. A needle! He had just shot me with something, some drug.

"Don't worry, baby, I got you," he whispered in my ear as the world around me faded to black.

TRIGGER
POINT

Again, to the reader, if you have a trigger for SA, please
turn to the next black page to skip the scene.
If not, turn the page and proceed.

~

Jessica

I woke up inside a small apartment that reeked like the inside of a dumpster. The scent of urine and alcohol was overwhelming. My head spun, but I didn't know if it was from the odor of the room or from whatever he had shot into my veins. The spot on my neck still throbbed from the injection.

My hair was heavy, caked with what I hoped was sweat as I lifted from the damped pillow beneath my head. I reached up to touch it but found my arms tied down. I could lift my head enough to see that my body was still mostly covered by the clothes I'd picked out before heading into work.

My pants were intact, but he ripped my shirt, which left my left breast exposed. I tried not to imagine what he'd done to me to leave the skin around my nipple raw, and instead focused my thoughts on a plan of escape.

The ropes around my wrists were not tight, and if done carefully, could be removed. I couldn't see much of the room. To my right was a small kitchenette. A pile of trash sat in front of the stove, likely the source of the stench. To my left was a door that muffled the sound of running water in what had to be the bathroom. That meant the door beyond the foot of the bed was the exit.

I had to get free. The rope on my left wrist was the looser of the two, so I started with that one. I did not pull; afraid I would tighten it. I moved my hand across the bed, pressing down and forcing the rope to slide. It was about to slip over my fingers when the sound of running water quieted.

I stopped moving, laid my head back on the pillow, closed my eyes, and waited. The door opened and allowed steam of the shower to escape. It freshened the air for a moment, but the pungent smell of the room fought back.

Heavy, wet footsteps exited the bathroom as my captor neared me. The moist heat lifted from his skin as he leaned in to hover just above me, allowing his foul breath to fill my nostrils.

"Mmm... damn, baby," he whispered before he placed a wet kiss on my forehead and left me alone again. Those heavy footfalls entered the filthy kitchenette, where he rattled around.

I hoped my presented unconsciousness would deter him. It did not. He returned to my side, sat on the bed, and hummed an unfamiliar melody that made my skin crawl. He continued humming for a minute before the sound changed from an uncomfortable lullaby to a disgusting groan.

It became more difficult to control my breathing as the panic crept over me. The bed shifted as he sat next to me groaning. I gave no reaction as he pawed at my raw skin. He pinched my nipple. The pressure felt like fire.

He groaned again as he shifted his weight above me, nearly crushing my chest before finding a comfortable position. He was on top of me with one hand on my breast and the other on himself. He pulled back my shirt to reveal my right breast.

"Damn. Amazing tits." His lips brushed against my neck and moved down to wrap them around my nipple. He alternated between the right and left, kissing, biting, and nibbling.

The motion of him stroking himself pressed against my leg. He whispered a name that was not my own, quickened his pace, and then his body jerked. The fiery liquid that escaped from him spread across my inner thigh.

Hope allowed me a moment to believe it was over, but it wasn't.

CHAPTER 2

"*Baby, wake up, please. I need you.* You called, and I came. Please, baby. Wake up." When I didn't respond, he groaned and punched the wall above my head. The unexpected impact made me flinch, and he laughed. "Playing possum, are we? Well, let's play a game."

His hands grabbed ahold of my shoulders before returning to my breast. He tore away what remained of my shirt and pressed against my stomach. With fingers wet from either the shower or the moisture his own body created, he traced small circles on my skin above my belly button.

Everywhere his fingers touched me, his rough lips followed. I remained still, but my mind raced. What would he do to me? How could I escape him?

My pulse quickened when his hand reached the only thing that kept me safe from him. The button on my jeans broke as he struggled to remove them and whispered his unwanted apology. His struggle resulted in success, and all that kept me separated from him was a pair of sheer panties.

My legs now bare, the cool air brushed across my skin and caused my body to shiver in response.

"Are you cold, baby? Let me warm you up." His fingers slid the thin fabric aside before invading my body. "Baby, you are so tight!" he groaned.

The absolute worst part about the experience was the unexpected reaction of my own body. Fear arrested me, and yet somehow, there was still arousal there. Something deep inside of me responded to his disgusting touch and made me question my own sanity.

"You like it, baby, yeah, so tight. Mmm, so moist." His weight shifted on the bed as he lowered himself until his chest was between my legs. He blew hot, moist air onto the skin of my stomach in small circles, and he traced the same path that led past my navel and down to the spot between my legs.

His voiced faded in and out of my mind, and another sound replaced it. A low hum, a familiar song I couldn't place. It was calming, yet sensual, and somehow terrifying.

His lips hovered above me for a moment, as if he was going to ask for permission to continue. He did not. First, I felt his tongue as he flicked my clit. I wanted to move, but I didn't dare. The flicks turned into strokes. Slow strokes that moved around, causing my body to tremor. The song inside my mind grew with intensity.

His fingers were still inside me. Two of them, dancing between my legs. I couldn't help it. I tried to fight it, but the moan escaped my lips. While it repulsed, my brain and my body were rejoicing. He stayed there, between my legs, for a long time, causing me to spin out of control.

"I want you, baby. I have to have you!" The weight of his body shifted as he positioned himself on top of me.

"No!" I yelled. I opened my eyes. For the first time, I could see him. Long dreads, full lips, and dark yet pale skin. There were those disturbing voids that stared back at me in that night. "Don't!"

"Don't?" He looked furious and somehow hurt. "Oh yeah, I am having you, baby. All of you."

"Please don't!" The tears that fell down my face were not a product of sadness. Fear was the expected emotion. The sheer desire to survive the moment. But I wasn't afraid. I was furious. Anger burned through my chest and mind. This man had no right to touch me, no right to look at me without my permission. My thoughts turned dark as I yelled at him to stop touching me.

He didn't listen, and I felt him as he pressed against me and tried to gain entrance. I shut my eyes tightly and wished I could stop him. Then I felt it in the pit of my stomach. For a moment, it felt like I would cave in on myself.

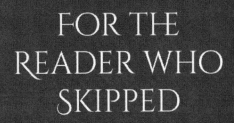

FOR THE
READER WHO
SKIPPED

I'm so happy you're here. Proceed for the safe part.

What happened?

After the attack, we find Sy in a bad situation, but she is
about to tap into a powerful part of herself!

With that feeling, the song in the back of my mind turned darker. It was no longer sensual, but more tribal, as the rhythm shifted from a lullaby to a chant of power. I had to open my eyes to see him. Something inside me forced me to witness what was about to happen.

Those dark voids bucked from his face, and he looked as though he was trying to move but could no longer do so. The veins on the sides of his neck bulged with his struggled protest of the invisible restraints.

He looked me in the eye and tried to say something, but before he could force the words to form, there was a new sound. The cacophony of bones breaking. Throughout his body, they snapped as if under extreme pressure. A tear fell from his left eye, tracing the outline of a small scar on his cheek. I watched it pause there, vibrating with the energy trapped inside his struggling body, and then he exploded.

I lay there for a moment, in shock and covered in bits of him. A loc still attached to his scalp laid across my stomach. My panic was a muted expression of tremors that covered my body. Crying or screaming may have invited unwanted investigators.

It was hard not to find relief in safety because of my confusion. There was no logical explanation for what had occurred, but I was safe from him. My brain shifted again to the one thing that mattered, my freedom.

I continued my original plan, pushing the rope over my hand until it released me. Once free, I located my bag, which of course didn't have the phone I dropped outside of my home. After searching through his belongings, relief came with the discovery of a beat-up cell phone in the pockets of a dirty pair of pants.

My last resort would have been to leave the apartment. My captor could do no more harm, but I didn't know what waited for me on the other side of the door. I pulled up the GPS and found the location, then called the police.

It took a half hour for the cops to get to me. The grips of panic released my chest when I heard them banging on doors down the hall. I unlocked the simple lock and waved them down.

After giving my recount of events, they met me with questions about my mental stability and drug habits. It wasn't as if I could expect any other response after reporting that the man who had abducted me and was trying to rape me spontaneously combusted right before he got the job done.

What I left out was the internal question that this was my doing. The song that played in my mind and the chanting. Had that done this to him? During the ride to the hospital, I debated asking if I could have been responsible, but decided that doing so would buy me a one-way ticket to the looney bin.

After the rape kit, drug test, medical counseling, and questioning from the police, I was free to go home. As I walked, I held myself, trying to stop the pieces from breaking free. I felt raw, not only physically, but mentally.

Hours spent being grilled by the cops, and I realized they wanted to make sure my story didn't change. They thought I was hiding something. As if I were protecting the person responsible for spreading lover boy's brains around the apartment.

I pulled the oversized police jacket around my shoulders. The stylish addition to my wardrobe came with a fresh pair of scrubs with a large stain on the left pants leg. I turned down the offer of being escorted by the overweight cop assigned as my temporary keeper. I swear I could hear his thoughts. Nasty vile thoughts about things he wanted to do to me. How he would love to touch me and taste me. It was all I could do to keep my Jell-O down.

They handed my belongings to me. Anything my attackers hadn't destroyed, or were free of bits of brain matter, in a small plastic hospital bag. They asked me to look through it, but at the time I couldn't care about anything more than making it home to my own bed.

Though the sun provided more warmth to the day, it did nothing to stop the icy wind that cut through the thin jacket. Still, that cold cut was just the thing to distract my mind from the pain in my wrists from the ropes used to restrain my arms, the tenderness between my legs from both his fingers, and the rape kit performed, and the way the world felt... different.

Instead, I focused on the memory of the faces of my attackers. The others who cornered me and helped him capture me. Those drugged up wastes of flesh.

Maybe one of them would attempt to use my credit card. If they so much as punched the numbers in on a keyboard, the cops would be on their asses. I wanted to remember every detail, from the dirty dread head, to the short one with no teeth. Funny, I didn't remember seeing any such details before, but now they were as clear as if I was standing in front of the chubby one watching him pop a piece of greasy chicken into his mouth.

A thirty-minute walk in the cold was enough to wake anyone up. I made it to my home just in time for the high dosage drugs the nurse pumped into my veins to wear off. I'd just about made it inside my apartment when the real aches and pains hit.

That monster had his way with my body and left me bruised and sore. At the time, adrenaline and the desire to be free blinded me to the extent of his abuse. The only solace I found was that he hadn't finished the job. According to the detective who spoke to me, often attackers liked the victim to be conscious, so my playing possum had likely stopped things from going further.

The first thing I did was strip away the borrowed clothing and hop in the shower. After listening to the doctor's report of the specimen found on my flesh, I felt filthy. He was still on me, and I scrubbed my skin until it felt raw. Still, I felt dirty and remained under the flow of water until it ran cold.

My bed welcomed my return, but I knew sleep was not an option. There was no way I could shut my brain off; no way I could escape the images burned into my mind. It wasn't just one man who'd done this to me. He had help from friends who cheered him on as he took away my choice. Their faces returned to me on a loop. Each one of them drooling with an eagerness to get at me, waiting in line for him to be done with me.

I got out of bed, pulled out one of my old sketch books, and with a detail I had never created before; I drew each of their faces, each one of those assholes, including the asshole whose face had exploded. In the darkest red I could find; I drew an X over his face. One down.

The activity proved therapeutic, as my mind felt quiet enough to allow me to sleep. I stuffed the papers in my drawer and popped two of my emergencies sleeping pills. Hell, this qualified as an emergency, and within minutes, I escaped the conscious world.

CHAPTER 3

"*A* *unt Noreen?"* I called out as I peeked into the window of my aunt's home. She lived alone in what was best known as a place where people go to die. That's right, a senior community, and I hated visiting her.

Not only did it take me over an hour to make it to the suburb, but it was like all the cruddy old men couldn't wait for me to walk down the street. They pulled their wheelchairs to their windows and ogled me. One, Mr. Patif, I think his name was, had the nerve to even pinch me on the ass. I knew that old age had a way of making a person more brazen, but some people just lost their damn minds.

I visited my aunt after replacing my cell phone. Yes, I searched for it, but it was long gone. The woman who used to be my best friend no longer felt like a companion. The moment I turned twenty-one, she changed.

She never called me, even though we used to talk every day. It made me happy to keep the distance because I didn't agree with her lifestyle. The thing about experiencing a life-threatening event was that you realize there isn't a defined amount of time allotted to us.

I could have lost my life. The first call my aunt would have gotten about me in months would have been one from the cops telling her only living relative had died. That was only if they ever found me.

As I walked through the streets of this little gated community, I was thankful that she was in such a secure location. There would be no car full of crack heads pulling up to her, drugging her, and doing unthinkable things to her.

As I saw her door, painted a bright red, come into view, I tried to calm my thoughts. I couldn't go in there with such darkness on my mind. I had already turned down the therapy treatments offered to me by the state. Allowing my mind to go down such troubling paths was no way to keep me off the happy couch.

Aunt Noreen lived in the very center of the community, fitting, as she loved to be the center of attention. I grew up watching her fanfare and laughing at her displays of over-the-top emotion. She was once a showgirl; she would always be a performer.

Her house was like the rest, small, quaint, and understated, at least on the outside. The town ordinance prohibited any cosmetic changes to the outside of the units. Little old people loved controlling people, even if they were other old people. Still, she convinced them to let her have her door painted candy apple red.

The inside of her house was a different story. I never knew how she did it, but it was like being transferred to another world. Aunt Noreen had cornered the market on all things fantastical and piled them into her home without it feeling like a scene from *Hoarders*.

After calling her name and getting no response, I knocked on the door as loudly as I could without alerting Mrs. Johnson next door. That woman was bitter and once threw a shoe at me because she said my music was too loud. My music, which I played on my headphones ten feet away from her home!

The door to Aunt Noreen's home was unlocked, but I wouldn't dare enter without an invitation. I barged in on her one time and one time only. The result of my unannounced entrance was an image that would haunt my nightmares for months to follow. I walked in to find her dancing to reggae music topless and on the lap of a thrilled old man named Kenneth.

There was something special about my aunt. At only forty-five years old, she secured the best spot in a super-exclusive senior citizen gated community. In all the years I'd known her, she hadn't made enough money to pay for six months in the place, but it was going on six years since she moved in.

I questioned her about it once. I was told to keep my nose out of other people's pots before it got burned off. That was warning enough for me.

It was five minutes before my aunt heard me knocking over what sounded like calypso music blaring from within. She opened the door, sweating and smiling. Of course, it was her cardio hour.

"Oh, Syrinada! I didn't know you were coming." She pulled me into a hug that cut off my air and covered me in residual sweat.

"Hi, Aunty." I choked as and struggled to breathe until she released me from her death grip.

"What are you doing here unannounced during my cardio hour?"

"I just wanted to see you."

"Well..." She stepped back and posed. "Take in the magnificent view, baby girl."

I smiled at her before going inside. The moment the door shut behind us, I lost all my nerves. I had more intentions for going to her home than to catch up on lost times. There were answers I needed. Though our relationship had seen closer days, she was the only person I could trust.

Instead of asking the questions that haunted me, I followed her into the living room and sat as she instructed me. She fussed as she went to retrieve drinks for us and commented about how she would have had food for us if I had given her a heads up before coming.

Outside of being fussed at, this was an ordinary visit with highlights of the new Zumba class she was instructing and talks of the silly old bitty down the way who complained about my aunt's young male visitors.

"That old heifer is just upset because she can't get anyone to take her to the Citizen's Ball next week." She mimicked the unsteady walk of the woman who walked on a mahogany cane. "I mean, who would want to deal with that nag all night?"

Part of me hoped my aunt would notice something was wrong with me. She'd basically been my mother. Shouldn't some part of her know that someone had hurt me? As usual, however, Aunt Noreen was too wrapped up in tales of her own life to consider my true motives for visiting.

It was six o'clock when I headed home. My bladder full of Aunt Noreen's specialty, a mix of apple cider and lemonade. I was more than happy to get out of there before her flavor of the month showed up. As I understood it, this one was a young firefighter named Tyrone who showed her how to slide down the firefighter's pole. I was pretty sure she intended the pun.

That night, I sat in my bed listening to the news blaring from the television in the next room. My apartment wasn't the magical wonder of my aunt's home. The awkward wall in the middle of what was a studio apartment qualified it as a one bedroom.

I'd downgraded from a full-size bed to a twin just to fit it in the bedroom. If I hadn't, I would have to perform daily acrobatics to navigate the room. The good thing was, I had just enough space to fit the few belongings I had. I grew up with my aunt. Thanks to her and her endless collections of knickknacks and whatnots, I had a minimalistic approach to life and personal possessions.

One thing I was sure was a contractor's oversight was that my bathroom was huge. Here I was in a wannabe one bedroom with a large Jacuzzi tub and his and hers sinks... not that I had any use for the "his" section.

The news was, as always, a downer. I leaned back on my pillow, listening to reports of women found in basements. Over the course of a few weeks, their bodies started turning up all over the place. The suspects were all men, which made me wonder if the trail had already gone cold for the men who snatched me.

Was there even a trail to begin with? That damn detective was too busy pondering my bra size to be worried about finding out any useful information. The sketch artist they said would help me put a face to the other men never came. I questioned if the fat ass had ever even called him.

Annoyed with the continuous reports of horror, I picked up the small remote and shut the television off. My body was tired, but my mind was not. Instead of trying to force myself to sleep, I returned to my desk. The top drawer held the sketches of those men, the ones I'd created. No help from the justice department.

I sat at the desk and stared at that drawer. Inside were the faces of the men who'd tried to take my life from me. Did I really want to look at them, to give a fresh coat of paint to the tattooed images in my head? My gut told me not to do it. Those images would be bad for me. Trying to avoid opening that drawer for the rest of the night would only drive me insane.

Too restless to sleep, I grabbed my leather jacket and headed out the door. The jacket was heavier than the thing I wore before, but still not the bear that remained buried in the closet.

Across the hall in an apartment like my own lived a girl who most days I would avoid, but if I needed to take my mind off things, I could count on her for an adequate distraction. Latasha was, in more ways than I would ever have time to explain, a mess!

She was one of those girls who boasted about her own high level of confidence, never realizing that women with that level of confidence didn't have to promote it to the world. It was something everyone just knew.

She had to have been one of the most insecure women I had ever met, but she would do everything in her power to make sure no one ever found out about it. I never had the balls to tell her she failed. Her insecurities somehow made her more bearable, more relatable. Though I didn't boast to deflect from it, I was also unsure of myself.

Before I knocked on her door, it flew open, as it did most times. Either she had radar, or she stood on the other side of the door waiting until I poised my hand to knock. She would fly out the door, knocking me over while raving about some fabulous party she on her way to. By even daring to knock on her door, I'd agreed to attend the party with her.

"Siren!" Yes, ironic, I know. She called me siren because she swore up and down that I was irresistible.

This was her opinion, and if you asked me, it belonged to her alone. I, in no way, felt as tantalizing as she claimed I was to the opposite sex. My typical response to this was to laugh and nod as she paraded around me.

"I'm so glad you're here! This party is about to be the bomb. Is that what you're wearing? I mean damn, you want guys to look at you, don't you? You should try to look a little more inviting. I mean, with that whole voodoo thing you got over men. If you made yourself appear willing, I'm telling you they would all come running, but no need. Having you there always increases my chances of snatching up some young thang. Mmm. Not that I need the help or anything, just saying."

She hadn't finished her rambling before she dragged me down the hall to the elevators. It wasn't often that I got to say much in conversations with Latasha. Her mouth ran a thousand miles an hour.

To be clear, I loved Latasha like a sister. She was one of the best people I'd ever met, and I counted myself lucky to know her. Yes, she could use a little work, but hell, so could I! The elevator doors closed, and within moments, Latasha was sprucing me up.

She pulled my hair back out of my face and up into a loose bun that felt too heavy. "Messy is the new sexy," she claimed as she opened my leather jacket to reveal the oversized T-shirt underneath, and of course, without asking, she altered it. A cut here, a tie there, and boom, I was presentable.

"At least you always rock the cutest jeans." She squealed and smacked me on the ass. I grimaced from the pain; still tender from the events I hoped to block from my mind. She didn't notice. Lucky for me, because that wasn't a conversation I wanted to have.

"You okay, girl?" After chattering for another ten minutes as we made our way to the train, Latasha noticed I hadn't said a single word.

"Um, yeah." I nodded and pulled my jacket tighter around me. "Just cold."

"Hmmm, must have been a wild one. I noticed you didn't come home the other night. Tell lover boy to ease up next time. I need my girl energized for our nights out!"

"Yeah, I'll do that." It was all I could do not to cry as the train pulled up and Latasha started her 'ready to party' dance.

CHAPTER 4

By the time the doors reopened, I looked as if I had every intention of going out for a night on the town, outside of shoes. Black moccasins, comfy. She asked me to go back and change them. I said no. Hell, by the end of the night, she would want me to swap with her.

We lived in Chicago. The south side, so hitting any decent spots meant driving, hopping a train, or a combination of both. We usually went to the triangle. Three corners: North Ave and Milwaukee, where the bars were free (usually), the drinks were cheap, and the taco stand was always open. Hell, a good taco would soak up any alcohol and give you fuel to continue to party hard. I had to admit; the tacos were really why I agreed to go out. I mean, partying was okay and all, but I loved me some tacos.

We arrived, and after a brisk walk from the train, we were standing in line in front of our favorite spot in the triangle, where we began our nights.

The music was jumping; they had the good DJ today, and the temperature had risen, so it wasn't as cold as it could have been on a January night. Latasha was still freezing her ass off in her stilettos, fishnets, and mini dress. Her hair was the only thing keeping her warm, long and flowing down her back. She bounced around to keep warm and repeatedly told me how she needed a drink.

It took about ten more minutes to get inside, but once we were in, we were good. We knew the bartender, a guy named Straught. Don't ask what was up with the name. I had no idea. We always ordered from Straught. His drinks were stronger, and he often gave us the five-finger discount. Little miss pouty face, also known as Alissa, was stingy with the alcohol, and I was pretty sure she overcharged. I guess drunken, horny men didn't really know the difference.

The night was the same as always. There were a lot more people out and about than you would normally see in January. Chalk that up to the random heat influx. Thirty degrees when we woke up that morning and sixty-five degrees at eleven o'clock at night. That was Chicago for you. Maybe that global warming thing everyone was yapping about was true.

Either way, it was a glorious night to be out. We bumped into a few other regulars of the area, a guy whose name I had never known, with his girl whose name I could never forget because her drunken friend would always end up on the curb outside of Empire Liquors screaming her name. "Becky! Becky, bitch... where are you?"

Malachi was there. He was always there. I questioned if he ever went home, but never complained about seeing him. Why? This man was a sight to behold. If I had not touched his skin and felt its warmth, I would have sworn the Gods made the man of stone-cold marble. What I meant by that was all that damn dancing and marathon running he committed to had sculpted his form into something worthy of the term thirst trap. Therefore, anytime I watched him from afar, I always wished I could have a little more. Well, needless to say, that would not happen. Hell, me and Malachi weren't even on the same planet. Yes, we were friends, but that was all. He was just a nice guy, which didn't hurt his sexy factor.

We found him in the cramped space of Empire Liquors; he was the owner. Every girl stared at him longingly. If they could, they would rip his clothes off and have him right there on the floor. Of course, they would have to get in line. I called first dibs. The guys looked at him as if they wanted to rip his throat out if they got the chance. Of course, they would have to make it past all the women. There was no way in hell we would let this fine specimen go to waste.

A description of Malachi? Okay, if I must. Six feet tall with nicely kept locs. Call me crazy, but I just loved me a sexy man with locs. Smooth skin like caramel that I was sure tasted the way it looked. He had that face, you know, the hard jaw line, soft eyes, and the classic face of a poisonous man. He looked as if he would chew you up and spit you out, but oh, you would enjoy the ride.

His eyes were a deep shade of green, a color not produced by contacts. I had scrutinized them often enough to know. Okay, I used the *contact check* to get closer to him. I mean, just think about it. How else can a slightly tipsy girl make sure your eyes are real, other than straddling you, pressing her breasts against your chest, and getting her face so close to yours the light could barely squeeze through the space between you? Hey, checking eye color was a serious matter.

Latasha walked right up to him, as always, snatching him away from the girl he was dancing with, some blonde haired, blue eyed, mass produced looking chick who tried to pull off a scary *bitch I'll cut you* look but ended up looking more like *why'd you go and do that?*

Latasha was in the middle of an extended hug when I grabbed my drink from Straught and headed over to join them. Malachi let go of Latasha, and as always, she held on for about five more seconds. I had to give the girl her props. Malachi waved hello, and as soon as I was close enough, he stole my drink.

Little blue eyes kept watch on us the entire night. She even followed us when we moved across the club. She did everything in her power to catch Malachi's attention, which was a complete waste of her time. Let's fast forward. I mean, you really don't need to hear about skimpy dresses, overly drunk idiots, and a puke fest from hell.

At some point in the night, Latasha disappeared off the dance floor. This was normal. I told Malachi I would look for her, and I moved away. When I looked back, the girls had already swarmed him. I laughed as I pushed my way through the crowd. Checking every corner of the club left me empty-handed, so I stepped outside; I could only hope she hadn't walked off with some guy.

The night air was alarming as I left the warmth of the club. I pulled my jacket tighter around me as I pushed past the drunken crowd. Twice, I dodged tumbling girls who drank a tad too much and once I had to jump out of a stream of vomit from a guy who was trying desperately not to embarrass himself in front of a group of hot girls. Yeah, let's just say he failed.

"Tasha!" I called out into the crowd. I caught the smell of tacos. The stand was open, and there was a line, as usual. Tasha loved their tacos too, so I headed over to check the line.

Tasha wasn't there. That was when I began to panic. What if something had happened to her? As the terror crept over me, I heard her; at least, I thought I did. My friend sounded confused or drunk. I turned to see the alley; the entrance to it was at the back of the line. I poked my head around the corner, and I saw him. For a second, I froze because I recognized him.

Yeah, he was cleaner, less grungy looking, but it was really him. Number three in my sketches. He was there that night when they snatched me from the street outside my home. I remembered him instantly, even though I only saw the side of his face. He had a scar right below his eye, and his skin had that same odd tint of gray, the shade of the sick and dying.

Then I noticed he was hovering over something... no, someone. The only thing visible were her legs. Then he shifted to the side, and my heart stopped. Latasha was lying on the ground. She looked scared, but mostly because she was too drunk to understand what was happening to her. He reached for her, and I felt my blood boil.

"Hey!" I called out to him, and he turned to me. "Get away from her!"

"And what are you going to do if I don't?" He stepped toward me, then stopped. "Oh, I remember you, the pretty one that got away." He laughed.

"Leave her alone."

"Or what? You haven't told me. By the way, how the hell did you get away? What happened to Rodney?"

"Would you like to find out?" I asked, and the bravado of my voice shocked even me.

"Oh, please, baby... show me." He grinned, flashing a mouth full of yellow and decaying teeth. His breath was strong enough to overtake the stench of mildew and garbage that lingered in the alley.

"I'll show you." The confidence in my strut as I walked over to him wasn't one that I recognized. It was as if my body was acting separately from my mind.

I approached him slowly, and he puffed out his chest. He was obviously driven by ego; he actually thought he was appealing. It was a sad display, and I felt my stomach turn. Somehow, I could survive his stench long enough to get close. I touched his face and brought him closer to me.

"Oh yeah, baby." He groaned.

I found it pathetic that just a touch got him so excited and that he believed I would allow him further access to my body. At least he preferred a willing victim to an unconscious one. I smiled at him and could actually taste his pleasure in the air. *All that from a smile?* I didn't question the fact that I was tasting pleasure or that I could almost see it coming from him.

As his body temperature rose, so did the heat around us. Waves of his desire pressed against me. Suddenly, I was hungry, but not for food, for his lust and his pleasure. Before I could stop myself, my lips were on his, and I was kissing him hungrily. There was zero resistance from the man who was now my prey.

His hands clawed at me and pulled at my clothing. His hips circled as he shoved his body up against me, and then he changed. Persistence fought with resistance as he tried to pull away and yet pushing himself further into me. *He wants me, and he wants to get away at the same time.* The thought paraded through my mind, exciting me on an animalistic level.

"Sy, stop!" I heard him behind me. *Malachi.* I released the man, and it was a moment before I realized he dropped to the ground when I let him go.

"What?" I screeched at Malachi. I was angry, and he had interrupted my pleasure.

"Look at what you are doing," he said calmly. His hands were up to show he meant no harm.

I turned to the man; he looked different as he lay on the ground in front of me. His body was withered and old.

"What the hell?"

"I will explain it to you later. Now, we have to get the hell out of here."

He picked up Latasha, who had passed out, and carried her out of the alley. I paused and stared at the man on the ground, near death and still reaching out to me. I turned and ran after my friends.

CHAPTER 5

M *alachi nearly chewed his lip off* as he drove us back to his place. I sat next to him in an impatient silence because I had questions, but I couldn't ask them. What if Latasha overheard something? Hell, what if she'd already seen something I had no hope of being able to explain? As terrible as it was, I hoped she'd been so intoxicated that it would wipe all memories of the night from her mind.

Besides having my drunken friend in the back seat, I wasn't even sure how to begin a conversation about what just happened. What concerned me was that Malachi didn't appear to fear me. He didn't run from me. He didn't call for the police. Instead, he offered his help. Yes, I knew we were friends, but hell, that was a lot to ask of a friend. *Please ignore the crazy ass inhuman shit I just did and take me to your house, so I don't get caught with the dried-out husk of a recently living man!* Yeah, I always aimed to be a good friend, but that was too much, even for me.

He said he would explain. What was there to explain? I was a monster. Was that what he would tell me? Only monsters were capable of what I had just done. Only monsters could enjoy it as much as I had. Was I something evil? The head explosion was one thing. I could write that off as a freak accident. I could blame it on the drugs my attacker was clearly high on. This, whatever had happened to that guy, happened because of me.

I didn't need Malachi's explanation to know it. I felt the life slipping away from that man, and I wanted more of it. What did that say about me? My mind raced as we sped down the interstate.

Malachi lived in Naperville. It was about an hour's drive from our hang out area. Whenever I questioned why he would come so far to party; he told me it was because that was where I was. I felt like he was just picking at me, just saying it to make me blush, a hard reaction that wasn't difficult to inspire. As the car pulled into the long driveway, I reconsidered whether there was truth in his confession.

He shared a large place with his older brother. Okay, to say they *shared* it was being nice. Malachi was basically a squatter there. His brother Demetrius was barely ever home, and Malachi reaped the rewards of a child with an absent adult. Although technically he was an adult himself, he didn't always act like one.

Demetrius was an executive, a self-made millionaire, who traveled most of the year. It was the perfect setup for Malachi. The arrangement meant that he rarely had to spend any of his own money. It wasn't as if Malachi had no money to spend. It was just another reason that men envied him and women wanted to get their claws into him. He was already on the path to being just like his brother.

The only time I'd been to his home before, I'd only seen the outside. We were picking him up for a party that was in Aurora. We all drove together and I, of course, was the designated driver. Malachi specified he had every intention to drink until he could no longer stand. He came out the door, clearly already inebriated. He told me he was just "a bit tipsy." This was as he tripped and almost fell right onto that gorgeous face of his. I remembered laughing at him as he fell into the car on top of Tasha who squealed before copping quite a few feels. I mean, her hand went directly to his ass!

Inside, the house was stunning. His brother had beautiful art lining the walls of the foyer, eclectic portraits of creatures of the sea. The theme continued throughout the rest of the home as well. Cool blues and mellow browns and an array of earth tones. It felt homey. Well, if your home was under the ocean.

I remained in the living room while Malachi took Latasha and laid her inside one of the guest rooms. I trusted him not to try anything with her. He was always the one to defend us against the creepier representation of the male species!

In the living room was a large sand colored couch that called to me. I melted down into it and stared at the ceiling. It was a high arch decorated with smooth stones. I counted the stones and made patterns in my head that were constantly changing. It wasn't long until I had zoned out completely, soothed by the colors and the warmth of the home.

I felt relaxed and secure. I closed my eyes, lost in thoughts of water nymphs, mermaids, fairy tales, and magical realms. For a moment, I wished I were one of them, free of the earth, free of assholes that tried to rape and kidnap girls, free of police who barely cared to catch them, and free of the unexplained madness that was taking over my world.

"Comfortable?" Malachi nudged my arm.

My head hung over the back of the couch. I opened my eyes to see his face above my own and wearing a bright smile. His long locs tickled the sides of my cheeks, and I smiled.

"Yes, this couch is like a dream."

"Glad you're enjoying it." He hopped the back of the couch and plopped down next to me. "Can I get you anything? Water, tea..." He smiled, knowing I would want neither.

"How about an explanation? The one you offered me earlier?" I sat up and turned to face him.

"Oh, right to business, huh?" He sighed, but the smile remained on his face.

"Yes, if you don't mind." The act of tiptoeing was for children. I had some freaky shit happening to me, and I needed to know why.

"Okay, well, obviously you may have noticed things went a bit awry tonight." He was easing into the topic.

"A bit? That's an understatement, don't you think?" I scoffed.

"Yeah, well, I can explain it to you. You may not like it or even believe it, but what I tell you will be the absolute truth." He spoke in a calm yet firm tone.

"I'll try to keep an open mind." How hard could it be to accept what he had to say? It wasn't as if the recent events were normal.

"Sy, you are a mermaid. A siren, actually." Malachi spit the word out as if they left a sour taste in his mouth. I thought he would laugh and tell me he was joking, but he didn't, he just stared at me.

"What?" I finally asked after a pause that felt like it would choke us both.

"Yes, your mother was one, and even your aunt is," he said, just as serious as ever. "Think about it. How else would she be able to date the guys you describe seeing at her house?"

"Right." I gave him the side eye.

"Look, I said it would be hard to believe, but I can show you better than tell you, if you let me."

"Okay." My palms suddenly felt like I'd slapped a slug. I rubbed them against my pants legs. "The night can't get much worse, right?"

Malachi got up from the couch and headed for a door at the back of the room. "Come on."

Yes, I was reluctant to follow him, but I wanted to see what he had to show me. Even though it sounded like complete nonsense, but so did exploding heads and men shriveling up from a kiss. I was hoping for something that would settle my stomach. I had little hope of that happening.

He pushed the door open and revealed a set of stairs that disappeared down into the basement. A metal chain hung from the ceiling, which he pulled firmly on and started the sound of gears turning. A light came on, and he walked down the steps, giving me more comfort as I descended the stairs behind him.

"What is this?" I questioned as I followed him and got that uneasy feeling in my stomach.

"A basement," he joked.

"Ha-ha. Seriously, what's down here?" I poked him in the back of his head.

"Some things that will help me with my explanation." He chuckled. "Visual aids, if you will."

The light reached no further than the bottom step. Malachi stuck his arm into the darkness to flip a switch that illuminated the space and revealed the large shrine that was set up in the center of the room. It was a complete museum of artifacts dedicated to underwater beings.

Malachi stepped to the side and allowed me the opportunity to take in the depictions of mermaids. There were photos and other drawings and paintings. There were locks of hair, and in a large case at the back of the room, what looked to be an actual tail! My wide eyes turned on his face as I struggled with the instinct to run.

"Okay...?" That was all I could get out of my mouth. He knew he needed to explain it.

"This is my bloodline. Sy, I am like you. *Merman,* I guess you would call me. My brother and I are the last of our line."

"The last of your bloodline, as in everyone else in your family is dead?" I felt bad for him. I knew his parents died, but not his entire family. Come to think of it, I never really heard him refer to anyone in his family before.

"Yes. They forced our people to flee from the seas because of a war between the witches and the sirens. Few survive the transition to land."

"Witches? Okay, slow down, please. You cannot just throw mythical, fairy tale dwelling creatures at me and keep talking like it is common nature." It was impossible to keep my eyes on him. There were so many things that called for my attention, including a skeleton of a creature I had no way to identify.

"You're right. I'm sorry." Malachi grabbed my hand, leading me to a small bench along the wall. We sat down and he began his explanation again. "Okay, let's start from the beginning. You know all the things you think exist only in fairy tales? Well, most of them are real. They aren't just stories meant to bring comfort or instill caution in children. We, our people, are one of those mythical species. You and I are sirens, or mer-people. The media mostly refers to our kind as mermaids. Our people were free, and they roamed the seas, ruled them. They were powerful creatures. The water was not only their home, but it was the source of their power.

"That power gave them the ability to do many things. Like creating new lives; new worlds inside the seas. They helped to keep the earth in balance. It also gave them the power to walk on dry land, but only for short periods of time.

"While they were on land, they discovered humans found them to be irresistible. They could make the land dependent beings do anything they wanted with just a thought and the sound of their sweet voices. This was not that terrible of a thing until the women fed. Something happened. Something changed.

"It wasn't everyone but certain siren women. They mated with and pulled energy from the humans. It started innocently, as most things do. They would pull a bit, get a little high off it, and go on their way. Then they discovered the energy lingered with them. It strengthened them and showed signs of extending their life expectancy.

"The witches, the ones we were unaware of, came from the shadows and banished the sirens back to the seas, but they were insatiable; they wanted more energy from the humans. They wanted to feed and become more powerful.

"Instead of returning to land and risking being caught by the witches again, they used their siren call to draw the men into the sea. It took little effort. The pull was intoxicating, not only for the human men but also for the sirens. It started slowly. One or two men, nothing to be too concerned about. They were smart about it; they drew the men in from scattered areas, and they would send them back with no memory of their experience under the sea and life went on normally. Until, once again, things went too far, and they pulled from the men their entire essence.

"They meant to kill them, to suck them dry of their life force. Some of the sirens felt this was too much to take. They fled to the depths of the seas to escape the wrath of the witches that they knew would come. Nevertheless, there were the ones who had no concern of the consequence. They figured with their newfound power; they would be more capable of defending themselves against the witches.

"It wasn't until a witch answered the melodic call of a siren. A male, he knew what it was; he recognized the sound, and he went to the siren. Her name was Mengali, and she was told to be a devastating beauty. He intended to kill her, to stop her from what she was doing. Instead, he fell for her. In time, Mengali took all the witch had to give. She left him a dried-out husk at the bottom of the sea. When this became known to the witch covens, they declared war.

"The fight lasted for a long time, on land and beneath the seas. Both sides lost countless lives. In the end, the witches called on the influences of their ancestors and their gods and used the power to strip the sirens of theirs. It was the ultimate punishment for their evil deeds. Only a few could regain it, and to do that, they would have to go through a tenuous journey to find their Siren Stone. It was supposed to show who was worthy of having that power, and hopefully eliminate those who would misuse it. However, in my opinion, those people would fight the hardest to get it. Either way, few would find it; fewer would survive."

"And what exactly is a Siren Stone?" My mind could process only so much, but the stone felt important.

"When a siren is born, a stone forms at the mouth of the Ononolo Volcano underneath the seas. If the siren chooses to, she must make the journey across the seas and find the hidden path to this volcano to retrieve her stone. Then and only then can she have her powers. The thing to remember is that power is not something you can destroy, but you can strip it away and transfer it to another object."

"Okay, this makes no sense. If I am a siren, and sirens do not have power unless they retrieve this stone, which I damn sure have not done, how do you explain what happened to that man in the alley?"

"I would say it happened because you are the daughter of a siren and the daughter of a witch. I guess technically the men are called warlocks, but that's splitting hairs again. The power that you have, however sporadic it may be, is because of your parents." I protested his announcement, but he interrupted me before I could say much. "I know you were not aware of this, but it is true, Sy. Your father was a warlock. Your mother a siren. It was a forbidden love, but it happened."

"And how do you know all of this?"

"Because they tasked my family with protecting your family, which means protecting you as well."

"And what about you? Did you find your Siren Stone? Is that why all the women love you and all the men hate you?" I left the daddy debate for a future discussion.

"No, I haven't, because it doesn't work that way for men. I have the power to attract women, but I do not pull from them. When the witches cast their spell, it was one that affected the women only. They were the ones who had the voice, the siren's call; they were the ones who possessed the power to pull the energy from humans."

"Awesome, not just the bitches who did the dirty, but all of us. Great."

"Yeah, it's unfair, I know."

"This is a lot to take in. There are so many questions I should ask you, but I can't seem to think of one. And I'm still struggling with the urge to run the hell out of here, because none of this sounds logical." I stood to pace the floor. "How can I deny what you're saying after what I've seen with my own eyes? Men withering away, heads exploding, it's all—"

"Heads exploding? Wait a minute now, slow down." Malachi left his seat and grabbed my shoulders, stopping my pacing. "What are you talking about?"

"Oh, right. I didn't tell anyone about that." I looked at the floor, suddenly feeling ashamed of what happened to my crack head abductor.

"You didn't tell anyone about what, Sy? Tell me." He stopped close to me. The look on his face was one of genuine concern; even more so than when he found me in the alley with Tasha and that man-raisin.

"Well, I was kind of kidnapped, and the man who took me was attempting to have his way with me, and... I don't really know what happened. He was on top of me, my hands were tied, and I just kept thinking that I didn't want him anywhere near me, that I didn't want him to touch me, and the next thing I knew, I was covered in brain matter. The police thought I was insane. Hell, I thought I was insane." Of course, I left out the details of how I was shortly turned on by that asshole. That would prove to be a concern. Especially now, a half siren, it could mean that I was one of the bad ones. He might have felt obligated to turn me over to the authorities. I wondered if they had siren police. How would they punish me for my transgressions?

Malachi pulled me into his arms. "I am so sorry, Sy. I had no idea. When did this happen to you?"

"Earlier this week." I shuddered because I felt odd. I was relieved to have someone else know, yet ashamed that any of it had happened at all.

"Are you serious? What the hell, Sy? Why are you out partying and acting like nothing happened?" He pulled his arms tighter around me, burying my face into his chest.

"I'm sorry. I just needed to get out." My words were muffled through the fabric of his shirt.

"No, don't apologize to me! I am just saying you should be in counseling or something, not running around with Latasha's wild ass."

"See a counselor and say what exactly? I think I blew up a guy's head with my mind. Oh, and return with the tale of how a man withered away into old age after I kissed him. Right, they would lock me up in a loony bin in no time!" I relaxed in his hold. "Besides, you know how persistent Latasha can be. Telling her no rarely leads to her not getting her way."

"I guess you're right." He abruptly released his hold and stepped back from me. "Let's go back upstairs."

"What? Afraid I might suck you dry?" I tried to make a joke of it, but it felt flat. It was how I felt. It hit me then that I may never be with a man again. I didn't have that much of a love life to begin with.

"No, not at all," he said, sure of himself.

"Why not?"

"Well, for one, I am not a threat to you. Something like that is usually a response to a siren being put in a dangerous situation. Typically, it's not intentional. And for two, it works a bit differently when you are with your own kind."

"What do you mean?" I raised a brow.

"Those men, the ones you... hurt. What happened to them only happened because you did not invite them into your space. You didn't want their hands on you. You didn't want their lips, their touch. You wanted nothing more than to get away, so you did." He paused and moved back over to me. "Now, say, if I was to touch you, caress you," he leaned into me and placed his hand on my cheek before slowly sliding his fingers down my neck. "You would not want me to stop. You would be open to me, you would invite me in."

"How do you know that?" My voice was a hollow sound, nearly absent, halting. He had me lingering on his every word, intending for me to know his every thought. *This siren shit was powerful.*

"I just know, Sy." He leaned in close enough to kiss me but didn't. "When you open your eyes to it, and you see what I see, you *will* invite me in. You will call to me, and I will answer you." He pulled away from me and headed back up the stairs. "Coffee?"

"Um, yeah." I swallowed the lump in my throat and stood at the bottom of the basement steps long after he disappeared through the door at the top. I had to wrap my mind around all he had said to me, as well as calm the tremors that began between my legs. What did he mean I would invite him in? What could he see that I did not?

CHAPTER 6

I *was finally home in my apartment,* with Latasha safely tucked away in her own place. After spending the night discussing fairies, witches, and mermaids in real terms with Malachi, I just needed to be alone. Malachi, of course, wanted me to stay. He wanted me to take him on as some sort of siren mentor, but after the intense way he talked about me inviting him in, well, I didn't see that as a possibility.

I couldn't, not because I didn't believe him, but because I did. I believed it all, and I didn't want to. I was the daughter of a siren and a warlock! It made absolutely no sense to me, no matter how many ways I tried to look at it. It didn't matter what my gut told me. After all, my gut hadn't always been the most reliable source.

It was Saturday afternoon, and I drew my curtains to block out the sun. The darkness soothed me and made it easier to focus my mind. What was I supposed to do? I was having a hard time jumping back into a normal life after what I had just learned. I thought about pulling out my teddy bear, my form of a security blanket, from the back of the closet, but that led me back to where it all began; a childhood of lies.

Then, I considered drawing but remembered the faces that inhabited the pages of my sketchpad. I rolled over on my bed and saw it lying there on the desk. The pad where I etched the faces of the men who kidnapped me and would have tried to kill me if given half a chance. Images pulled from my personal horror movie memories. Two of those men were dead now, and it was because of me. It should have scared me to know I possessed the power to do such things. I should have been terrified that I could take a life so easily, but it gave me a strange sense of satisfaction.

I got up because remaining in bed and contemplating life just wasn't enough. Not anymore. I needed to know if what Malachi told me was true. Forget the gut feeling. I needed solid evidence. I threw on my clothes, hopped into my car, and drove to my aunt's retirement community. When I got there, I pounded on the door until she came to answer it, frazzled and pulling on her silk robe.

"Girl, what is wrong with you? Is everything okay?" She peered out the door and looked over my shoulder as if someone or something might have been following me. I pushed past her and entered the house, unable to hold in the questions; unable to beat around the bush.

"Are you a siren? Am I?" I blurted out.

"What?" She tried to sound as though the question was completely nonsensical to her, but I saw it all over her face. The truth. The recognition. She didn't have to respond. She didn't have to say it. I knew the truth.

"You are, aren't you? So was my mother, and so am I!" I paced the floor. The calm acceptance I had experienced when discussing this same topic with Malachi was long gone. Now, I felt it all, the anger, confusion, and frustration. Each emotion was vivid and intense. I wanted to reach out and hurt someone, anyone.

"Syrinada, baby girl, slow down. What are you—"

"Stop it Aunt Noreen! I know the truth. I have seen things. I have done things, terrible things that I have no explanation for, and you stand here in front of me and try to pretend? Be real with me, because I want to do those things, those terrible things, and I know it is because of who I am. It's because of *what* I am!"

"Slow down and talk to me." My aunt held her hands to me, coaxing me to comply.

"No! Admit the truth. Now!" I paused, but she didn't reply. "Are we sirens?!" I demanded.

"Yes." She dropped her head, almost as if she were ashamed to admit the truth.

"Why didn't you tell me?" I pleaded with her. I wanted to know the truth, yet I still hoped it all was a lie. I wanted to somehow erase from my mind everything that had just been revealed to me.

"I promised your mom I wouldn't. I had to protect you, Syrinada. It was up to me to keep you safe."

"Protect me from what? Were you going to protect me from the witches; from their council?"

"How do you know about that?" she asked with a sick expression on her face.

"It doesn't matter. Why would you need to protect me from them?"

"Not them, Syrinada. The witches are not my concern." Her face turned red as she continued. "It is your father."

"My father?"

"Yes."

My saucy aunt led me to the back of her yard, a small space filled with exotic plants that released their sweet fragrance into the air and gave the yard a feeling of being detached from the world around it. However, at that moment, I could not enjoy it or use it as the escape I usually would. I was only concerned with where the hell she was taking me and what new insanity was about to be revealed. I had been in her shed before. There was nothing in there but gardening tools and bags of fertilizer that released a stench you would spend the next five hours trying to remove from your sinuses. A complete contradiction to the gorgeous flowers and the hypnotic scents it helped to create.

As we entered, I almost questioned her. I almost asked her if she had lost her mind. Almost because she ducked down, pushed aside one of those stinky bags, and revealed a door that lay underneath it. She lifted the covering, which opened to a set of stairs that disappeared beneath the floor of the shed.

"Well?" My aunt looked at me and motioned for me to go down the steps. "Go on. You want to know the truth, there it is."

"You want me to go first?" I asked her, and I could see the hurt on her face.

"Nothing down there is going to get you, girl. Go." She scoffed. "Don't trust me suddenly?" The question felt more like a challenge, a test of some sort.

"Do I have a reason not to?" I asked as I moved down the steps into the darkness. As I stepped down, I felt a strange nudging in my center. A feeling that made me feel like this was a big mistake.

The room below was much like the one Malachi revealed to me beneath his home. The only difference was it was not as brilliantly lit. It held artifacts of our family; the ones lost in battle and old age. This included my own mother. At the very center of the room was a small podium. On it, there was a picture of my mother. That was all there was. Nothing more was left of her, just a simple photo!

"Where is the rest?" I turned to my aunt, who wore a home-sick expression.

"What?"

"My mom, where is the rest of her stuff? I have seen this picture before. Where is the rest of it?"

"We lost it, Syrinada, to the seas."

"How? How could everything left of her be lost?"

"We had to flee our home when the witches found out about your mother and father. They saw their union as an abomination. Once they found out about you, they sent their henchmen to come and destroy our home. They had every intention to take our entire family down with it, including you! Can you believe that? What kind of monsters would seek to harm an innocent child?"

"So, they killed my mother?" I ignored the idea of an entire race of mythical beings wanting me to die. I had enough to worry about.

"Yes," she answered simply.

"But not my father?"

"No, not him. I am sure they would have, but he was no longer around. He had been long gone by then. Things between him and your mother, well they didn't work out as she had planned."

"So, my dad left me, and witches murdered my mom, and you took care of me?"

"Yes, and it wasn't easy. I had to be sure they couldn't find you. I couldn't afford for us to pop up on any radars by looking too suspicious. We had to blend in."

"You did all of this with help from the Denalis?"

"Who?" She frowned.

"You know, the Denali family. The ones who were hired to protect us." How could she not know them?

"I have never heard of a Denali family." She shook her head and waved off the thought.

"Well, my friend is one of them, and he helped me. He said that his family has been responsible for watching out for ours and making sure we've been safe for years."

"This is the first time I've ever heard of them." She shrugged. "Of course, the power that be often acted without consulting anyone. I wouldn't be surprised if there were more people watching and waiting than your Denali family."

"Doesn't seem like they were very good at their job, considering what happened to my mom."

"Well, as I said, I do not know them. You need to be careful of who you choose to associate with. You never know who can truly be trusted. Even those who you would consider the closest to you should be suspect."

"Even you?" I didn't know why I asked or why I couldn't seem to stop myself from doing so.

"Especially me," she said with a smile, as if she intended it as a joke, but there seemed to be something else there. Whatever it was, it started that nudge inside of me again. I realized right then that my aunt was someone I wasn't sure I could trust. She had lied to me and kept things from me, and I couldn't elude the feeling that she was leaving out a lot from her story. I was sure the information she had conveniently left out was without a doubt the information that would truly change the way I looked at her.

"So, tell me more. I want to know about our family. Everything I thought I knew, the vague details. They are all lies, aren't they? Is my name even Syrinada? I mean, it sounds mythological, I suppose, but is it really my name?"

"Yes, I suppose I should tell you your real name. Syrinada is in fact your name, but the last name Jones doesn't belong to you, at least not by birth. Yes, compared to Syrinada, it is a very simple last name, but it's the one given to us when we could finally come out of hiding, and I just couldn't bring myself to change your first name. Your mother loved it, and luckily, few people know what your name was. Your mother and father were very private people, and anyone who truly knew you died in the raid.

"Your actual name, the one given to you at birth, is Syrinada Alia Sania, daughter of Siliya Alia Sania, granddaughter of Sulia and Notha Sania and niece to me, Noreen Mali Sania. They considered our family royalty beneath the seas. There were a few families like our own. They were the ones who sat at the top of the food chain, so to say.

"Unfortunately, the ones who committed the treachery that led to the sirens being stripped of their powers were from those families. There were five families, to be exact. The women of those families committed crimes that went far beyond luring human men to their deaths. The men of those families cleaned up their messes and created cover stories, but there was only so much the men could do before things got out of hand and they could no longer hide the truth. Word quickly spread of their carelessness, and sometimes, their cruelty."

"Was my mother one of those women?" I asked. "Did she hurt people?"

"Oh, no, this was long before our time. Those women were a different species altogether. They were fierce and hungry for power. They are the creatures they based all the myths on. Your mother just swam up to the wrong pier at the wrong time. She let her heart lead her, not her gut instinct, and that was her biggest fault."

"So, crimes, war, and death. Does that about sum up our family history?"

"Well, of course there is more, but basically, yes. At least the part that seems to count right now. Of course, we had our enjoyable moments. Our family survived simply because our female ancestors were not okay with taking the lives of others. It was asking too much. They were not there when the witches first struck and fled to the open seas. An informer told them what was to come, and they left. They tried to warn the others, but they were all drunk on stolen energy and thought themselves to be unstoppable. Our ancestors feared the witches and knew of the power they could wield. So, they left. They left them all behind to be destroyed."

"Sounds like they at least tried to help them."

"Yes, I suppose so."

"You think they should have stayed and fought?"

"I think they would have been stronger together. You should never leave your sister behind."

"Well, what about my mother? You two were there together. How did you get away, and she didn't?"

"Your mom hid us beneath the reefs. The only thing she was concerned with was protecting you, and she entrusted that to me... She told me to take care of you and make sure you weren't harmed. I begged her to come with us and hide, but she knew they wouldn't stop until they found her. I heard her; she told them your father had taken you, but they didn't care, they killed her anyway.

"I waited as long as I could before I ran with you. I had to go through so much, but I brought you to safety, as I promised your mother I would. It wasn't easy, Sy. It wasn't easy leaving my sister and all the other people I loved behind, but I did it. I did it for your mother and you!"

"Look, I am sorry. I didn't mean to be disrespectful. I... just... this is a lot to take in. My entire life has been, well, not my life. It was fabricated by you, and I am not even sure who else. How can you not understand how I feel?"

"I didn't think this would be easy for you, which is why I never told you. I meant to so many times, but I didn't think it was safe or fair to tell you about a life and a world we could never return to."

"Yeah, well, it seems like it was more selfish than anything. You didn't want to have to deal with a stressful situation. I don't think it would have been that bad, not if I had known all along. Not if you hadn't kept it from me for so long."

"You're right, and I'm sorry. I just chose what I thought was best. What I thought would protect you."

"Look, I need to get out of here." I stepped around her to get to the stairs.

"And where are you going to go?" Noreen asked.

"Does it matter? I need to leave." I looked back at her, pausing my exit. Part of me wanted her to give me a reason to stay, a reason to trust her.

"Okay, then go." She nodded and turned to adjust one of her precious things.

"I will contact you soon. I just really need to figure this mess out. Not that I have any idea of how to do that."

As I left her house, I kicked myself for thinking that my aunt could show me compassion. Our relationship had changed so much since I became an adult. In the four years since my twenty-first birthday, my loving aunt had become just another stranger on the street who I didn't know if I could trust.

CHAPTER 7

Have you ever found yourself just walking, not knowing your destination or even having any recollection of how you got to your current location? One moment I was driving away from my aunt's house, contemplating the utter pile of shit my world had become. The next, I was walking through the same dilapidated neighborhood that the cops found me in after my incident. I scoured the streets, looking, searching. But for what? I walked by broken homes and faces of lost souls, and I couldn't care at all. I could see their sorrow and pain, and it meant nothing at all to me.

When I saw him, I knew exactly why I was there. He was standing outside the corner store laughing with an overweight man who punched him in the arm and headed off down the street. This nameless asshole, one who I can't forget, croaked out a hollow laugh. His ugly expression, oversized nose, and scarred jaw were recorded along with the rest of his drug addicted pack on the pages of the sketchpad that still lay on my desk. Those his eyes locked in my direction, but it was as if he didn't see me. He became nervous and abandoned his chosen spot in the corner. *Maybe he thinks he is just tripping, coming down from his last high.*

I followed him, making no effort to hide. He watched over his shoulder, looking directly at me as I trailed him. Still, I got the feeling he could sense my presence but couldn't see me. He kept walking, and each time he looked back at me, my nostrils flared as a pungent scent filled my head. It leaked from his pores and created a trail for me to follow. Even when I lost sight of him, I knew where he was.

I was not myself, but I reveled in the change. Following him felt nothing short of predatory. I felt my body purring as I moved and loved the feeling. The scent of his fear mixed with the other odors in the decrepit neighborhood worked to excite me. His perspiration carried the adrenaline in his system. Fear and drugs were a powerful mixture. Fear must have taken over because suddenly he broke out into a full out run. I didn't chase him. There was no purpose to it. I knew exactly where he was.

Following his stench led me to a tall, rundown building. An abandoned project that was now a dank shell that had a terrible odor that worked to turn my stomach. Trash and feces of both the animal and human variety covered the streets surrounding the building. There were old men and drug addicts laid out on stoops, grumbling about things unknown. Young kids, whose mothers were probably out selling their bodies, were playing alongside the building. They saw me and smiled. I waved, and they waved back.

For a moment I was myself again. All I could think of was how much I wanted to take them away from that terrible place, but that wasn't an option. The cool breeze brought the scent of my prey back to me, reengaging the animal inside of me. I turned from the innocent eyes that watched me and headed into the building. The ass had run up the stairs. I followed his odor up eight flights. The scent led to an apartment, five doors to the left of the landing.

A thick layer of grime and bodily fluids covered the walls of the disgusting hall. The smell of sex and drugs clung heavily in the air, and I found myself aroused. *Why the hell was I aroused by this?* I questioned my physical response to this environment, but I ignored it. Ignored the tightness that formed between my legs and the way my nipples hardened beneath my shirt. I ignored the way my mouth watered, and my pulse quickened. I dismissed it all and focused on his door. The one marked with the broken 8E.

The door sat partially unhinged. Great for privacy, I was sure. I barely touched it, and it swung open to a small room. There wasn't enough of it to be called an apartment. There was just one small room, no bathroom, because of the shared locker room style lavatory at the end of the hall. In the left corner was a small burned-out hot plate. Likely used for other concoctions, which had nothing to do with the culinary arts.

My eyes landed on my scented target, cowering in the right corner on the floor, his body shaking like a leaf in the wind. His eyes darted around the room. He knew I was there, but he couldn't see me. I wondered why this was, but once again, I ignored it as my inner predator roared.

"Who are you, and why are you here? Leave me alone!" he shouted.

From the opposite side of the thin wall, I heard his neighbor yell out for him to cool it. "Stop fucking with that mixed shit, man, and shut the hell up!" He followed his complaint with a pound on the wall.

I laughed because the idea of it was amusing to me. He heard my laughter and looked in my direction.

"Who are you?" he asked again and squinted as if he still couldn't see me.

Newfound frustration outweighed arousal. What good was it for me to be there if he couldn't see me? He needed to know who I was and recognize why I was there. I wanted to witness the moment he realized when he had made his mistake. I bared my teeth and growled, and he fell back into the wall.

"It's you! What the fuck did you do to me? How did you get into my head?!" He stood up, clearly able to see me. "Please, I am begging you, man. I'm sorry."

"Please tell me what exactly you are sorry for." I stepped forward; a grin of satisfaction stretched across my face. This was what I wanted. His fear. His regret.

"You, know, I don't know... everything. We do some fucked-up shit when we're high. We shouldn't have fucked with you like that. It wasn't right. I'm sorry!"

"Come here!" I demanded, and despite his terror, he complied with my command.

His legs carried him to me, and his fearful expression glazed over. All his anxiety slipped away from him as he approached me. His hands slowly lifted, and he reached out to me. In a matter of seconds, his focus shifted from apologizing for attempting to rape me to trying to fondle me!

"Do not touch me!" I spit the words at him, as if they could burn him on contact. He groaned and pouted. "You're disgusting!" I felt the anger boiling inside of me, the rage that accompanied my sentiment. I let those feelings pour from me and fill the room. He reached for me again, and my only thought was a single word, burn.

The anger I released in the room compressed around him, and he screamed, which elicited a round of yells from his agitated neighbor. As he fell to his knees, flames forming around his arms, I turned and left the room. I didn't care. Not about him or the people in the building who ran past me as the fire engulfed the room and spread out into the hall. The sad-looking children along the street, no longer fazed me, but the chaos aroused me. The sweet delicacy of fear enticed me as I left the building.

The last thing that registered as I walked away from the blaze was the heat on my back. One moment I was staring at an old man lying in the street, and the next I was pulling my car to a stop in front of the snow-dusted lawn of Malachi's house. I stumbled from the car and swallowed hard. My body burned with desire. I was on fire, and I needed him. Only him; his name echoed inside my mind as if it were yelled into a canyon. I needed him.

My fingertip had barely pressed the doorbell before it swung open. I didn't ask questions. I didn't make sure it was safe. Hell, there could have been a crowd in the house, but I didn't care. My hands wrapped in the locs that hung around his startled yet knowing expression and pulled him into me. Instead of resisting me, he leaned into the kiss and growled as he pulled back.

"Sy, what the—" I didn't let him finish. I didn't want to hear what he had to say. I didn't want to face any of the questions he would have, nor did I want to process what I had just done or was still doing.

I pushed him back into the house and kicked the door closed behind me as I pulled my shirt off. "Strip!" I commanded, and he did as he was told. I watched him closely as he stepped out of his pants and quickly pulled away the T-shirt he wore.

His flexed muscles and an intense expression revealed how much he wanted me. Even though he stepped back, putting distance between us, I could feel his body thrumming with building energy. He presented himself to me, proudly, muscles wrapped in a smooth bronze coating that I couldn't wait to sink my teeth into. My mouth watered at the thought, and I bit my lip. I couldn't take it anymore, nor did I have the strength to pretend to resist him. Fuck playing hard to get.

I left the doorway, my breathing heavy with my own heat as I tried to contain what I felt building inside of me. It was an echo of the same energy that radiated from Malachi. With each beat of my heart and rise of my chest, I felt myself transforming into something else. Once again, my logical mind battled with my primal mind. Again, I let the primal side win.

"Sy," he spoke my name, but I shook my head.

If he talked, I would have stopped, reconsidered my actions, and probably retreated. I couldn't allow that, not with the way my body felt. To walk away now would be pure torture. Instead of having a discussion, I wrapped my arms around his neck and lifted my legs to straddle his hips and looked him in the eye. Malachi understood the urgency of my need for him. Large hands cupped my ass and supported my weight as our lips met.

Never had I kissed a man so deeply and felt my body respond the way it did to him. This was more than a kiss. It was a connection that reached to the base of my pelvis and pulled from me all the lust I had pinned up inside. An explosion of adrenaline ripped through my body. When our lips parted, I cried out, the agony of passion unsatisfied.

Malachi answered that cry. He lowered me to my feet, took his time in removing the final layers of my clothing, and lifted me back into his arms. His lips took a new task of covering my jaw, neck, and chest in kisses that left radiating sparks of energy behind. I hadn't noticed our movement until he lowered me to the couch. The cushions cradled my body, and his hands left my ass to cup my breast.

Thumbs flicked each nipple, stimulating my arousal as his tongue traveled past my belly button. He continued his path south until his face disappeared between my thighs. I squirmed with pleasure as he alternated between flicking my clit and diving inside of me with soft swirls. The combination sent me over the edge once more, leaving his face covered in my essence. I grabbed him by his locs, bringing his lips back to mine so I could taste myself.

Not relenting on his task, his fingers replaced his tongue, this time simultaneously stroking my clit and strumming my g-spot. I kissed him, pulling energy from his lips as my body rocked in another orgasm. His hands gripped my waist as the heat of his arousal met my own. Without pause, he entered me in one slow push until the tight walls of my sex fully captured him.

I could feel myself tightening around him, holding him in place, and his eyes met mine, heavy with desire. As my walls gripped him, he pulsated inside of me. This moment was something I never experienced. The focus, the intent, the heat that grew between us, and something inside me rejoiced. I placed my palms on the side of his face, bringing him closer to me, and kissed him first. He groaned, thankful for the gift of my lips.

We kissed until I could take it no more. The building fire had my head hot and my pussy throbbing.

"Malachi," I spoke his name in a heavy whisper.

"Yes, Syrinada," he answered.

"Fuck me," I commanded.

The hungry growl rumbled through his chest before the devilish grin spread across his face. He pulled away from me just far enough that his head teased my hole before going to work.

My back arched, accepting each powerful thrust. I emitted a quiet call as he filled me repeatedly and tears slid down my cheeks. He stopped for a moment, assessing me, and our eyes met. The moment was too intense to interrupt with words. A silent exchange was all we needed. Inside, I knew it meant more to him; I could feel the weight of the moment. He understood this connection in a way I was not yet capable of. Questions were for a logical mind, and at that moment, I was anything but logical.

Our eyes remained connected as he moved inside of me. Slowly at first, allowing me to appreciate the feel of him. As he sped up and moved deeper inside of me, the sensation became too intense. I lifted, pushing him back to the floor, and straddled him. I looked down on the man between my legs, his locs spread around his head on the floor, and I saw the light in his eyes. It was magical, and it added to my pleasure.

Though I wanted to watch the light that danced in his eyes, I slammed my lids shut as the heat formed in my belly and traveled up to my throat. I opened my mouth, and the sound that erupted from within me was not one I had ever heard before. It was beautiful and melodic. It rang out around us, filling the air, and Malachi sighed as his body tensed beneath the weight of my own. He gripped my hips and shuddered as he neared his climax. I opened my eyes to see him as he cried out his finale.

His eyes were closed, but when they opened again, I realized I was not the only one who'd changed. Malachi was something different now. He radiated power that fed my soul. And before I could move, I felt him stiffen inside me again. And again, I allowed him to ravish me.

CHAPTER 8

The pounding on my apartment door woke me from
my dream of an underwater volcano that spewed lava
and boiled the surrounding water. It was a vague memory that
faded as soon as I forced my heavy limbs to carry me from my
bed. I might have tried to stop for a moment to remember it,
but the rude ass pounding continued, and all I could think of
was mimicking the action on the face of the person responsible
for the sound.

"I'm coming, damn it!" I stumbled across the apartment to
the door and nearly tripped more times than I cared to admit.
My body felt almost too relaxed; there was good reason for it. I
smiled as I remembered the feelings I experienced earlier in the
night. That smile was immediately erased from my face when I

finally made it to the door. I snatched it open to find a furious Malachi on the opposite side. A nosy ass Latasha stood behind him, trying to peek over his shoulder. He shoved his hand into the pockets of his leather jacket before he spoke to me.

"What the hell, Sy?" He huffed at me. "It took you long enough to answer the door. You care to explain what happened?"

"Hmm, let me think. I was sleeping. It's not a new concept. What is there to explain?" I responded, agitated that he had turned my mood so sour, so quickly.

"Don't play dumb with me. It's not cute. You come to my house, fuck me, and then leave without a word. I went to get you a drink, and I come back to an empty room. You're telling me none of that deserves an explanation?" Malachi looked hurt; more than hurt, he looked betrayed by me.

I weighed my words before responding. I owed him an explanation, but how could I explain to him something I couldn't fully comprehend? My actions were primal. I hadn't planned it; it just happened. When it was over, while he had gone to grab a towel and water, I freaked out and left.

"What?" Latasha squealed from behind him, practically bouncing in the hall, completely overjoyed with the level of dirt he had just dumped into her happy little lap. It wouldn't be long before the entire world knew what he had just spit out. Her squealing erased any remorse I had felt for my actions as I pictured the chain of gossip with my name passed along the lips of the snide little bitches Latasha often hung out with.

"Ugh, come in!" I opened the door fully so he could walk through and slammed it behind him.

I could hear Latasha yell out, "I want details!" just before retreating into her own apartment.

"Explain," he growled again.

"What exactly do you want me to say? I couldn't help my-self." I laughed, but he didn't look amused. "Malachi, nothing is going to happen, okay? I told you I am fine. You're worried about nothing. You seriously need to calm down." I stepped back from him and waited for the look of disappointment to leave his face. It didn't.

"Calm down. Right. No problem! How the hell do you ex-pect me to calm down when you won't even tell me the truth, Sy?" He paused his agitated pacing. The halting movement looked like a child stamping his foot to me. Boys and their tantrums; how very annoying.

"What truth are you referring to?" I crossed my arms and waited for him to clarify.

"You know damn well what I am referring to. Do you think I'm a complete idiot? You did something. Something wrong, or you wouldn't be working so hard to avoid the question. Tell me!" His hands remained stuffed inside his pockets.

"What?" Who the hell was he to come into my home and accuse me of doing anything wrong? "Are you serious right now? You wake me up to accuse me of doing what exactly?"

"That reaction, your sudden arrival at my house, it's because you did something you shouldn't have done. How long are you going to play this game?" He shot me a knowing look that made my skin crawl.

"And how could you possibly know I did anything at all?" I challenged his theory.

"Because it drained you, and you needed me to help you recover from it!" he snapped at me.

"What are you talking about?" I felt fine before and after seeing him. Okay, so yes, there was a little boost afterward, but that was a common side effect of great sex.

"Yeah, it's one of those things I asked you to stick around and learn. A siren cannot work her magic without having something as a source to fuel it!"

"And you're trying to tell me you are that source?" I laughed. "Come on."

"I am your kind. We are the same, Sy, so yeah. If you were to have done what you did to me to someone who was human, you would have killed him. Hell, I could barely stand up after it. That's why it took me so long to come here."

"I'm sorry." What else was there to say? I had drained him, but he looked fine. I would have to be more careful next time around.

"Never mind apologies. That is not why I came here. I came for you to tell me exactly what you did today." He was back to his accusations; didn't even miss a beat.

"I just had a busy day." This time I looked away. It was getting harder and harder to lie to him, and I couldn't understand why. "I told you there is nothing for you to worry about."

"Busy like hell! Do not continue to lie to me!" he growled again, and I caved. Something inside of me broke, and I could not hold out. It was as if he commanded the truth from me.

"Fine! If you must know, I did something. I went and found another one of the slimy bastards who hurt me. And yes, I killed him! Are you happy now? You know the truth!" There it was, out in the open, my truth. And as the words registered, now spoken aloud and not just a thought in the back of my mind, I froze.

I was a murderer. It was my intent to harm him when I went to find him. What other reason could I have possibly had for going back to that area?

"You killed a man?" Malachi asked, and I nodded.

"Yeah, I mean… I think so." I clutched my stomach, suddenly feeling sick. "What the hell? Why would I do that?"

"Syrinada, this is why I wanted to help you with this. You don't understand the power you have."

"The sick part about it is it wasn't me. You know? It was me, but it was almost like I was on autopilot, just along for the ride. The things I did, they're impossible, or at least they should be. I haunted that man, Malachi, and then I took his life, and I enjoyed it! Every moment of his fear brought me joy. I enjoyed watching him burst into a ball of flames, fall to the floor, and dissolve into a pile of ashes! And it brought me relief to know he was no longer in this world. I felt a piece of that security, that peace of mind that *they* stole from me, come back. I don't want to be a murder, Malachi, but am I supposed to feel bad for that? Am I supposed to feel sorry for that asshole?"

"Sy—" he had already switched gears from accusing me to attempting to comfort me. I didn't want his comfort or under-standing. I wanted him to leave. It would have been different if he had come there with even a semblance of understanding.

Instead, he was there to scold me and make me feel like shit. Like that was what I needed as my world was being torn apart.

"Look, I am well aware of what you are going to say to me right now, okay?" I held up my hands to stop him from interrupting what I had to say. "It's wrong, it will change me, it will bring me trouble, and you want to help me. I get that, but you cannot possibly know how I feel right now. Please don't waste your breath pretending like you understand because we both know you don't."

"You're right. I can't say I know exactly what you are going through. Okay? That much I can admit, but what I know is how to help you make sense of what is happening. I know how to make sure it doesn't take you over." Malachi stood in front of me with pleading eyes, and it bugged me.

He looked at me as if I were something he needed to fix. As if I was a bomb to diffuse before it took out all of Chicago. I wasn't about to sign up to be his little DIY fixer upper. I would figure out how to control what was happening on my own and without him showing up and throwing his judgments in my face.

"Who's saying I don't want it to? How do you know I don't enjoy being taken over?" I lied. I was too much of a control freak to enjoy losing myself in that way. "They paid for what they did to me and for what they probably did to so many other people! The law wasn't doing shit about it. As if what happened to me was any priority to them. So now, I don't have to wait for them to sit on their asses and let those monsters continue hurting other people. If you ask me, I just solved the problem!"

"You cannot possibly mean that. I saw how it affected you after what happened in the alley with Latasha. I saw how frightened you were. You don't enjoy hurting people, regardless of how much they may or may not deserve it. That is not who you are." He stepped closer to me, and I stepped back.

"That's because I didn't understand what was happening. You would be scared too if suddenly you had powers you thought were fictional. Now, I know. I understand what's happening. Now, I can make sure they all pay for what they did to me. They deserve it!" My anger bubbled to the surface, and it felt good. It felt much better than it should have.

"Do you? Do you really understand? Forget the assholes that hurt you for a moment and tell me what you understand. Do you understand what happened between us back at my house? Tell me, Sy. Tell me what you understand."

I was afraid to answer him. He looked angry. More than angry. He looked completely enraged. If I answered incorrectly, I feared he would have attacked me.

"What do you mean?" I stumbled with my response. "We had sex. I mean, I know it was odd, but it was sex." Before I could finish the thought, my gut told me it was the wrong response. It was more than sex. I knew it meant more to him, even if I couldn't understand why. I knew it as it was happening.

It was more than a physical pleasure. I hoped I would never have to face it, that he wouldn't call me out on my shit, but he was. He wasn't going to just allow me to brush it off. That wasn't his way.

"Sy, that was not just sex! You came to me and used me to restore yourself. That isn't something you do with just anyone. You ciphered energy from me. That's something you only do with your mate!"

"My mate?" I scoffed at the idea. "What the hell are you talking about?"

"Like I said, you don't understand any of this." He shook his head.

"Malachi, I am not—" I started, but he lifted his hand to stop me.

"I realize this isn't something you knew about, and I do not expect you to be my mate, but you need to take your time and learn about this side of you. Had I been someone else, the way you did what you did, it could have meant your death.

The males of our species are not docile, though they do not possess your siren power. They are territorial creatures. Their strength fuels the female population. It is literally the battle of the fittest. The females fight for the stronger male, and if a male feels betrayed, used, or in any way harmed by a female, he can and will kill her!" He spoke with a jaw clenched so tightly it was a surprise the sound of his words made it through.

"Is that why you came here? To kill me?" Once again, my anger rose with the supposed threat. My instincts told me it was time to defend myself. I never thought I could feel that way about him, but there it was. Yeah, sure, I would invite him in. Those were his words; that I would invite him in. I did it, and now he wanted to kill me for it. *What an asshole!*

"No, I came here to protect you, or at least try to!" he growled. "But you are just so damned stubborn!"

"Protect me from what?" I ignored the insult of my character.

"Obviously, you're the one I need to be protecting everyone else from, since you insist on constantly putting yourself in harm's way! Not to mention, all the people, who you know don't want you to exist." He sighed. "I know you went to see your aunt. I know she explained things to you. Have you so quickly forgotten the warnings I am sure she gave you?"

"And how do you know I went to see my aunt?"

"I told you before. It is my job to know." His chest puffed out, proud of his successful stalking.

"So, why didn't you know where I was, or what I had done? You're so all knowing; how did that slip by you?" I teased him, which may have been a mistake, considering the way his face turned a light shade of red.

"Because you cloaked yourself. You were on our radar, and then you weren't. Not until you showed up at my door."

"So, if I don't want you to know where I am, you won't be able to find me. That's handy," I snipped at him.

He rubbed his eyes with his hand, controlling himself before he spoke again. "Not that I think you understand how you made that happen, but try not to disappear too often, please."

"What now?" I crossed my arms. If I had known how to cloak myself from him, I would have done it and left him standing in the room alone. "You come here, ready to knock my door down. I'm okay, you see that, but that clearly wasn't the reason for your visit. What now?"

"Now, you come with me, and you allow me to take care of you and help you through this."

"Come with you where?"

"To my house, Sy. Where else?"

"Hell, for all I know, you could mean the sea!" I sat on my bed and considered his request. "I don't know about that. You want me to come to your house? For what, training sessions? I don't think I am up for that commute."

"Good thing you won't be commuting. Pack your bags," he commanded, as if I would actually obey him.

"Excuse me?" I watched as he searched my small home for luggage, ready to pack my belongings for me.

"You need to come and stay with me, Sy." He disappeared into my closet and emerged with a large duffle bag. "You need to let me help you."

"I don't *need* to do anything. Stop telling me what I do and don't need." I walked over to the door and swung it open. "Let me tell you what I need. I need you to leave. I need to get some sleep, and I need to figure this mess out on my own!"

"You can't mean that. You don't know—" he started in on his almighty speech again, but I cut him off.

"Yeah, I know. I don't know what I am dealing with or how to handle it. I got it. Whatever. Go!"

"You have completely lost your mind." He tossed the bag to my bed.

"No, I haven't! But I am pissed off, and it is time for you to leave."

"This is crazy. You will call too much attention to yourself! There are always people watching, waiting for someone to fuck up. What you did today was a major fuck up, Sy!" he scolded me as if he hadn't done that enough already.

"Are you done now? Did you get it all out of your system?" I rolled my eyes.

"No! Far from it. Trust me!" He looked like he was moments from going over the edge, and I was so very tempted to administer the final push.

"Look, why should I sit back and play the victim when I have the means to get revenge on the assholes who thought it was okay to hurt me? There are so many out there just like them! They don't care about the lives they mess with, why should I be so concerned with preserving theirs?"

"So, what now? Are you going to fuck them all to death?"

"That is so low!"

He knew I hadn't gone to that level, and to accuse me of it was like stabbing me in the gut. Especially considering they had every intention of doing it to me.

"It's the truth! So what if you haven't taken it there yet? Do you think that makes you special? This is all new to you, and just because you haven't done the worst yet, doesn't mean you won't! You're pushing the limits, Sy! This is how it starts. You know that, don't you? Yeah, you have great intentions now. Trying to save the world from asshole drug addicts. It always starts for a good cause. However, the power and the magic that naturally flows through you are addictive and overwhelming. It takes over and changes the person who wields it. It always does!"

"How can you even say that?" I challenged him. "You act as if this is something you know about. But, again, I'll remind you, you don't. I don't need you to be my guru, Malachi. Like it or not, I am the one dealing with this, and I will decide how that happens. Not you."

"How? Fuck it. You don't believe me. I will show you!" He lifted his hand and carefully removed the necklace he wore. He handled it as if he were afraid it would break. "Take this." He handed me the thin leather cord with a small blue stone painted to look like an eye hanging from it.

"What is this? Why are you giving this to me?" I examined the stone and saw no reason for it. Until I looked up. I kicked the door shut behind me as I witnessed the beginning of his transformation.

The guy who had a way of making my cheeks heat and my stomach do flips changed. His body rippled with magic, and his skin darkened with every passing current. Moments later, he expanded. While his body became more of a physical imposition, his face took on a permanent sneer, a devilish smile filled with razor-sharp teeth.

His chest rumbled with deep growls as he changed, and when he finished his transition from man to beast, he stood and watched me. I wanted to speak, but I couldn't. I didn't know what would happen if I did. *Would he attack me? What if this necklace did more than just manage his appearance. What if it also was the key to his sanity?* I held on to the thin chord even tighter. If that were the only thing that would put him back to normal, I had to protect it. There was no one there to destroy it. No one except the beast that stood in front of me. I backed away from it until the doorknob pressed into my back.

"This is how I know." His voice made my chest tighten. This rumbling sound didn't belong to the man I knew. "I am the living result, evidence of a siren who lost her way. My mother was like you. She started out trying to do something good for the people. An attempt to make the world a better place, but it changed her, as it will you. The more she used her power, the more lost she became, because of her foolish belief that she could control it. My conception was nothing that should have happened, but it did, and she is no longer alive because of it."

"Look, I—" I wanted to apologize, but what was the point? What words could remove the foot so securely place in my mouth?

"Don't bother." He snatched the charm back from me and carefully replaced it around his neck. I cringed as his body cracked and caved in on itself. He groaned and bit his lip as he tried to hold back the cries of pain. I looked away because transforming back was obviously much worse for him. Moments later, he was back to the person I recognized and wiping the sweat from his brow. "Sy, you cannot do this, okay? Resist it, or it will change you. I cannot let that happen to you."

CHAPTER 9

***M**alachi left when he realized* I would no longer discuss the matter with him. All I could do was stare at him, waiting for him to flip out or transition back to the beast. Like my prey in the rundown building, fear gripped my body in its icy clutches. He spoke, but his words didn't register. When he walked by me to exit the door, I flinched. I backed away from him and refused to look him in the eye.

Not two seconds after he shut the door behind him came incessant knocking. I knew who it was; Latasha's nosy ass coming to get details about what she'd heard. Well, she would have to wait. I was in no mood to deal with her or Malachi, especially after what I had just witnessed. *What the hell was that?*

How did he expect me to react after that? *Who the hell did he think he was?* I mean, I was happy to have him on my side. I recognized it was a good thing to have someone who understood what was happening with me, but I didn't need his judgment. Things between us changed when I went to his house, but it damn sure didn't give him the right to tell me what to do. *Fucking men!*

On top of everything else that scrambled my brain, Malachi was something more. And whatever the hell he'd turned into, it sure as hell wasn't friendly. The dark energy still moved around the room long after he left. I lit the bundle of cedar and cypress that sat on my window seal and used the smoke to cleanse my space. I never bought into it before, but a friend from work got me a kit as a birthday present. This was the first time I felt a difference in my home after using it.

Latasha finished her string of curses that she shouted from the hall and slammed her door loud enough to shake the walls. She would get over it. The next time we went out, I would be sure to make it up to her. Maybe I would really amp up my siren side and get a few more fellas to look her way. With Latasha, that was enough to solve any problem.

I pulled my covers over my face and waited for that soothing blanket of my subconscious to roll over me. Unfortunately, each time I closed my eyes, my body trembled as my mind fought with unwelcomed visions. Malachi appeared to me, but not the way I would have preferred to see him.

Instead of the attractive illusion I knew, he would appear as what was apparently his *real self*. A product of my own transgressions. His eyes pleading with me to come with him, to learn to control myself, and when I would deny him, he would charge at me with the purest look of rage. It was hours of tossing and turning before sleep finally took hold of me.

I wish I could say I had pleasant dreams, but I didn't. I dreamt of myself crawling up the side of a volcano. The heat of the surface was agonizing as it burned my skin, and my flesh pulled away from my body each time I pushed forward. I continued, regardless of the pain, even as I choked on the ash and sulfur that filled my lungs. Something inside me screamed for me to keep pushing forward, so I did.

I was nearly there, at the mouth of the beast, when I laid eyes on the thing that called me. Power made tangible as a smooth pink rock that glowed with an inner light. No matter what I did, I couldn't deny its call. It floated just above edge of the mouth of the volcano. Flashes of light brough more heat as the lava within bubbled. *Keep going!* The voice inside my head urged, so I did.

The closer I got to it, the brighter it glowed. When I finally made it to the rim, most of the skin on my body was blistered or had melted away. Still, I got to my feet, and I smiled as I felt the hunger pull inside of me. This power belonged to me. I could feel it compelling me as I got closer to it. It would make me whole again. It would fix everything that was broken.

I reached out for the small stone and stood on my toes as I stretched myself out and over the rim of the volcano. As my fingers grazed the smooth surface of it, I could feel the pulse of its power, but it was a brief taste. The vortex of power grabbed hold of me, but it wasn't the stone. The strong suction came from below and pulled me down into the mouth of the volcano. I could smell myself burning, but I didn't care. As the last of me melted into a thick stew inside of the pot of hot lava, I was still reaching out for the stone.

Escaping my dream, I found my body drenched in sweat. The smell of sulfur still a potent presence in my nasal passage. Without urgent knocking at my door to distract me, I recalled every detail of the dream, and I wished like hell I could erase it from my memory.

I touched my face and checked my flesh. There were no bruises or burns. Which was a relief, because I didn't need to add another problem to deal with. Dreams that spilled over into reality would have been the perfect cherry atop an already highly dysfunctional desert. Did I need to be more of a cliche?

Already there were daddy issues, a life that was a total lie and a super-hot guy trying to fix me. I had read this story so many times, and each time I would turn the page and thank the powers that be that I would never be that girl. But there I was, sickeningly disturbing dreams and all.

A shower felt like the best course of action I could take. A quick glance at the clock, and my jaw dropped. I picked up my phone and checked the date. A full day had gone by, and the clock read ten p.m. This display also informed me of the ten missed calls and seven unread text messages. All from Malachi and Latasha. I also had one email from my job, which I ignored.

As my mind fully woke, the shower became less appealing. Instead of heading for the bathroom, I grabbed my gym bag. Suddenly, I felt energized in a way I knew wouldn't allow me another moment of rest. There was only one way I could think to burn off the excess energy.

There was an all hours gym near my apartment. Great for night owls like me. I hoped a long run and some weights would help me dispel some of the energy. The gym was the only thing I could think of that would help me with the way I felt. Well, there was another activity I could think of that would help, but that activity and the person it involved were currently off limits!

Arriving at the gym, I found an almost empty establishment. There were a few late-night runners on the treadmills, but not much more than that, not that I was expecting much. I checked in at the front desk with Michael, a gangly boy who was barely awake and looked at me as if I had committed a crime by showing him my ID. He rolled his eyes as he punched in my numbers on the small black card and then waved me off.

I dropped my stuff off in the locker room and stretched a bit before hitting the treads myself. After a quick twenty-minute run, I felt great, but the energy I hoped would have died down had only increased. I decided to move on to weights, I needed to work on my upper body strength. I wouldn't call myself a weakling, but I was no heavy hitter either and with the way my life was going, I figured I would need all the strength I could get.

Just as I finished my third set of bicep curls, I sensed him. Completely out of sight, but the smell of his cologne cut through the sweat of the others. I felt the heat from his body the moment he walked through the door. A wake-up call to that part of myself I knew little about.

I clocked his movement through his scent. First, he stood by Michael, lingering there. Perhaps the attendant was friendlier to the male visitors, but then I could feel his agitation. Apparently, Michael was just as attentive to him as he was to me. Agitation shifted to arousal as he walked past the treadmills where another woman ran.

I lost it as the full scent of him reached me just before he disappeared into the men's locker. It was a deep scent of earth and heat. I dropped the weights and walked away from the station, leaving my water bottle behind and would have left my phone as well, had I had not strapped it to my arm. The urge to find this man, whoever he was, was a powerful one.

I barely noticed the side-glances I got from the women, who for whatever reason looked as if they wanted to strangle me. Odd, because before that moment, they hadn't even noticed me. The men in the room, the few that were there, had stopped completely. Their bodies froze, but they locked their eyes on my movement. Even Michael had come out of his slumber long enough to stare at my ass. I noted the changes that occurred in all of them and ignored them as I continued the path that led me into the men's locker room.

He was in there, but he wasn't alone. There were two other men changing into their gym wear. They both stopped moving as I entered. They watched me as I walked over to the tall man; his bare back was to me. All I could see were long braids that draped down and hung heavy against the strong-muscled contours leading down to his ass! *Oh, what an ass.*

"Leave," I spoke, and the two men did as they were told. One let out a soft moan of disappointment as he did.

The man turned to me, and my arousal reached a new peak when I took in the sexy image that was presented to me. Smooth, deep brown skin covered his chest where there was just a dusting of soft curly hair. He didn't speak, and I didn't want him to.

"Come," I called, and he moved. He said nothing, but he did as I wanted. I became more aroused with each step that brought us closer to each other. My hand lifted to touch the curls of his chest, just as he bent down and lifted me into the air.

His hands cupped my ass as I wrapped my legs around him. An image of someone familiar, a moment just like this, flashed through my mind, but I quickly pushed it out of my head when his mouth met my neck, and his tongue drew circles across my flesh.

"Sit," I ordered, and again he complied. He sat down on the bench next to the lockers and lowered my feet to the ground to stand between his legs. Once sitting, he waited for further instruction.

"Undress me." I looked down at him.

As he pulled the layers from my body, he followed his hands with his lips and his tongue. He mapped the curves of my frame and tasted the salt from my skin. He groaned as he continued. When I was completely undressed, I stepped back from him.

"Strip." I pointed to the shorts that hid him from me.

I tucked my hand between my legs and allowed my fingers to dance between the folds of my pussy as he put on a quick yet seductive show for me.

Once he was completely nude, I moved to the bench, sitting with my legs open. I beckoned him to kneel before me. He knew exactly what I wanted. The smile stretched across his face just before he revealed a tongue long enough to touch the bottom of his jaw. His knees met the floor just moments before his lips and tongue found their target between my thighs.

I clutched at the sides of the cool metal as I tried to contain myself. Never had I been so thoroughly devoured before. His tongue not only wrapped around my clit in spirals, but it reached so far into my pussy that he touched my g-spot, and when he reached it, he made it his home. I crashed multiple times, screaming out to no one repeatedly as he wrote the alphabet with his tongue on my spot.

After my fifth orgasm, he reached into his bag, pulling out a condom. Not to let my excitement fade, he returned his tongue to my clit as he put on the protection. I was mid climax when his face left my pussy, and in one swift motion, he lifted my ass, wrapped my legs around his waist, and entered me.

As his dick slammed into me, everything stopped. Power, sex, magic all filled the moment, and my body felt as light as air. My head rolled as the combination took me away from the inside of the locker room. That energy, that insatiable feeling, I recognized it for what it truly was. Hunger.

Time froze, and I heard it, that voice that belonged to me, the version of myself that was supposed to be dormant. It took over the moment. I fought to regain control, but not before I heard him. It wasn't the voice of the man who was stroking my insides and sucking my nipples.

It was Malachi.

"Malachi!" I called out his name as another orgasm rolled across my body.

"Sy, stop." Malachi's voice returned an urgent request.

"No, don't stop," I said, closing my eyes and imagining him between my legs. My hands wrapped in braids, and I pulled him closer to me.

My legs tightened around him as he continued, giving me exactly what I wanted.

"Don't stop," I repeated. "Malachi," I called his name again.

"Don't do this," he pleaded.

"It feels so damn good." I moaned and prepared myself for another explosive climax.

"Mm, yes." The unfamiliar sound broke the vision I had in my head.

I opened my eyes and was reminded of my position. In the smelly gym room with a stranger between my legs. His lips wrapped around my nipple, and I almost closed my eyes to return to the vision, but then he looked up at me, and there were the signs of what I'd done written across his face.

Eyes that were dark pools of brown now appeared flat and greyed. Even more, I witnessed the smoky essence of his life slipping from him. It hovered around him, a visible aura. But each time I took a breath, more of it left his side, and I could taste it as I claimed it as my own.

This man was dying between my legs, and he had no concern for his own well-being. He continued his work to fulfill my desire for him. I watched in horrific pleasure as he withered. His muscled body lost tone, his skin paled, and he kept putting in work, now teasing my clit as he continued to thrust between my thighs.

Despite my desire to continue, I pushed him away from me. His body slammed into the locker, and he paused for only a moment before he staggered forward in hopes to continue his work. Blood dripped from his nose; he crawled across the floor, reaching his hand out to me.

"Stop!" I yelled, and he did. Naked and sitting on the floor at my feet, he was a statue, an ode to his former self. Though he stopped, there was still desperation in his eyes. It looked as if he would cry. "Oh, I - I'm so sorry." I quickly pulled my clothes on and left him sitting there, rock hard and waiting for more. I'd never made it out of the gym so fast in my life. If anyone was staring, I didn't notice.

I drove to my apartment and grabbed the empty duffle bags out of the closet. I tossed in a few essentials and some items I felt I needed to have with me, like my sketch pad and laptop. I skimmed the room and made sure I wasn't leaving behind anything of importance. It wasn't as if I would never return; I hoped. I locked my apartment and stared at Latasha's door for a long while before deciding it was best not to say goodbye, at least not until I knew what it really meant. This time, I drove with a clear head to Malachi, and this time, he was waiting for me.

CHAPTER 10

"I *don't even want to know* what you were doing."
Malachi stood in the open door as I approached, with
my bags hanging from my shoulders.

"Okay, I won't tell you," I responded. I knew I was in the
wrong, but he didn't have to go into attack mode. "You want to
help me out here?"

"I take it you plan on staying a while?" He tilted his head and
nodded at the bags with a sarcastic smile.

"Yes, if the invitation is still open." I stared and waited for
him to step aside and let me into his house. He did not. "Okay,
maybe it isn't." When I turned to leave, he stopped me.

"Of course, it is," he called after me in defeat. Malachi looked at me like wanted me to fight him for it, plead for him to forgive me and take me in. *Yeah, good luck with that!*

"I'm sorry." I gave him something. No, I would not beg, but I was wrong, and I was big enough to admit that much.

"And what are you sorry for this time?" There was the judgement again.

"Seriously?" I rolled my eyes. "What happened to you not wanting to know?"

"Just come in." He finally stepped aside and let me enter the house.

"You know what happened, don't you?" I asked.

"I don't know what you mean." He hung his head and pressed his forehead against the closed door.

"So, that wasn't your voice I head in my head?" My bags dropped to the floor as I waited for him to address me. I needed a serious response from him. No matter how much animosity existed between us.

"It was. So?" His bruised ego was a monument standing between us.

"So, I am sorry. I didn't know." I tried to keep the sour attitude out of my tone.

"There is a lot you don't know, but it doesn't seem to stop you from acting so reckless. Remember, you got this, you don't need me!" He turned to face me, the anger now clear in his expression.

"That's what I said, but I was wrong." I nodded. "Is that what you want to hear?"

His body flexed with tension. As upset as I was, and as hard-headed as I could be, something spoke to my more submissive side, and I felt myself soften to him.

"Yes, you were. What did you do this time?" Malachi's body relaxed the moment he noticed I had given up the fight. The corners of his mouth turned up slightly, and I wanted to slap the smirk clean off his face, but of course, I did not.

"You don't already know?" I let the sarcasm bleed into my voice. Just because I didn't physically slap him didn't mean I didn't want my words to sting.

"I know you were with someone. I know you were taking his energy, and I know he was human." Malachi gritted his teeth as he spoke.

"Okay, so what else is there to tell you? You seem to know it all." I crossed my arms over my chest in defiance of the dominance he clearly wanted to have over me.

"Did you kill him?" A simple question weighed down by the expectant disappointment. He already told himself I'd done the worst thing imaginable.

"No... but I came close. Too close." I dropped my head because I knew if it hadn't been for Malachi's cries, that man, whose name I still didn't know, would have died.

"And now you're here." Malachi relaxed completely. His tension eased, knowing I hadn't harmed an innocent person.

"Yes. I didn't know where else to go. If you'd like me to leave, just say the word." I stood in the hall waiting for him to drop the ax. Instead, he sighed and held his hand out to me. I picked up my bags from the floor and handed him one. "Thank you."

"Don't mention it." He grabbed the bag from me, and for the first time in far too long, he smiled at me.

"So, what happens now?" I tossed the last bag over my shoulder.

"Now, I suppose we go to sleep, considering it is the middle of the night." He pointed to the staircase at the end of the hall.

Malachi led me up the stairs to the guest room. On the way, we passed by his bedroom, which he quickly pointed out to me, and yes, I tried to peek inside, but the door was not open far enough. I could only see the edge of his bed and the covers that were tossed on the floor.

"This will be your room." We stopped at a room two doors down from his. He pushed the door open and motioned for me to go inside.

"Thanks." I sat my bag down on the bed and plopped down as well. I expected him to come inside, but he dropped the duffle bags at the door, said good night, and walked away.

I sat there dumbfounded as I listened to his footsteps carry him further away from me and into his room. At least the door didn't slam when he closed it. I told myself that was a good sign.

I considered unpacking my bags but left that task for the morning. My clothes fell in a pile next to the bed before I climbed beneath the comforter. Despite the bed being perfectly comfortable, I couldn't get to sleep.

Each time I closed my eyes, I saw the nameless man in the gym. Each moment of our encounter replayed in my mind. It was the hungry look in his eyes, the weight of his body on top of mine, the heat of his thighs as he thrust inside of me.

Whenever I broke from the dream, I opened my eyes to find my hand, my fingers dancing between my legs. I would pull back, get up and walk around the room to cool off, and then try to sleep yet again. This was my night, a constant cycle of waking up and cooling down, and heating back up again. The sun rose as my temperature finally reached a normal level.

I continued my efforts to sleep until the sound of movement came from downstairs. Malachi was awake. My mind immediately went to places I knew I should steer clear of. A repeat of my last visit to his home. He could feed me with his body, and the cycle of sexual frustration would end.

I couldn't do that to him again, though. Clearly our last experience wasn't something he enjoyed, and I refused to hurt him again. Yes, he'd become a judgmental pain in the ass, but he was still my friend. I opted for a shower. Lucky for me, the guest room had an adjoining bathroom, which meant I wouldn't have to leave the room and risk running into Malachi while my hormones were trying to take over my mind.

The warm shower was supposed to ease the tension in my body and give me control of my brain again. That was not what happened. Instead of relaxing me, the water had an odd effect on me. I thought the pulsating shower head would relieve the building tension in my muscles. Instead, I felt as if I had plugged into a charger. I felt more awake and more alert as the invigorating water rolled across my flesh. The water was turning me on. I slapped the shower wall with one hand and muffled my frustrated cry with my other. I couldn't be around men, and now apparently showers were off limits as well.

As outraged as I was, I didn't stop. It felt too good. I remained beneath the flowing water, because, well, I couldn't *kill* water. When I put my back to the stream, I felt a lover's caress that slid down my back and cupped my ass. I turned around and the warm flow became the lips and tongue of a man in heat. He played with my nipples, teased them, and drove me wild before dropping between my legs to sample the taste of me.

By the time I climbed out of the shower, horny wasn't enough to explain how I felt. There wasn't enough walking, exercising, or mental caresses of an invisible man that could calm me down now. I hadn't allowed myself to reach that peak in the shower. I couldn't be sure Malachi wouldn't hear me and scold me for the action. How the hell could I explain an orgasm via a stream of water?

He judged every action I'd taken so far. That wasn't one I wanted to defend myself for. My body still dripped with water as I paced the bedroom floor. What was I going to do? Was I meant to live the rest of my life blinded by my sexual desire? Soft taps on the door interrupted my frantic thoughts. Startled, I tripped on the inconvenience of air but caught myself on the bed before hitting the floor.

How embarrassing would that have been to have him rush in and find me on the floor with my ass up and nothing but a towel on?

"Yes?" I said and tried not to sound too shaken.

"It's me," he responded softly. I hadn't even considered that it would be anyone other than him.

"Okay, give me a second." I scrambled up and grabbed my bag.

"Is everything okay?" he called through the door when I didn't open it.

"Yes, everything is fine. I am just getting dressed."

"Are you sure you're okay?" he asked again.

"Yes, I will be down in a minute!" I yelled as I struggled to pull my panties over damp skin.

No response but the sound of heavy footfalls walking away from the door. I hurried, getting dressed, and attempted and failed to calm myself before I exited the room and journeyed downstairs.

The smell of eggs and bacon filled my nostrils, and my stomach growled. I couldn't remember the last time I had eaten food, but I didn't care. Eating seemed unimportant. The world was all mermaids and dead guys. No time to think about such basic things as food.

Malachi sat at the kitchen counter, stuffing his face. Another plate set next to him under a glass cover. When he noticed me, he nodded at the plate and invited me to join him.

"Breakfast? Thank you. I'm starving." I sat down next to him and pulled the plate over to me.

Though I felt hunger, food wasn't what my body craved. I tried to focus on the meal in front of me, but being near Malachi was completely overwhelming. Maybe I could play off my excitement as enthusiasm for scrambled eggs and pancakes. My hand trembled as I removed the covering from the plate.

I took a deep breath, trying to refocus my desires, but instead of the aroma of food, the scent of his skin filled my nostrils. My mouth watered at the memory of the taste of his skin. He took a sip of his juice, and when he pulled the glass from his mouth, there were droplets of juice on his lips.

Out of the corner of my eye, I watched his tongue retrieve the drops, cleaning his lips, and my thighs squeezed together with anticipation. My short fuse had finally burned out. I couldn't take it anymore. I hopped down from my seat and slid between him and the table, blocking his access as he reached for his fork.

"What are you doing?" He leaned back in his seat.

"I'm hungry." I growled at him, and he flinched. Of course, it turned me on even more to see his reaction to the more primal side of me.

"Well, your food is on your plate." He nodded to the untouched meal that sat on the counter.

"That isn't exactly the appetite I am trying to satisfy right now, Malachi." I grabbed the collar of the blue T-shirt he wore, pulled, and groaned when the fabric ripped easily.

The sight of his chest drove me wild. I wrapped his long locs around my fists and pulled. His head fell back, and he groaned as my lips touched the skin of his neck. My teeth grated against his flesh as I teased him with nibbles along his collarbone. I lifted my legs and climbed into his lap before I claimed his lips with my own. Just as I sunk my teeth down into his bottom lip, he pushed me back.

"Sy, stop!" The sound of his voice was a mixture of a growl and a moan. It was a warning, and yet an invitation.

"Why?" I whined.

"Learn to control yourself. You can't just pull from me like this," he spoke in heavy breaths and held his grip firm on my shoulders to keep me from proceeding. He licked his lips, and blood dripped from where my teeth had pierced his flesh. The sight of it was oddly erotic for me, and I licked my lips. I wanted more.

"Why not? You can handle it." I launched myself forward, and the weight of my body sent the chair and us flying backwards

We crashed to the floor, and despite his pained expression, I locked my thighs tightly around him and kissed him. He gave into me for a moment. His hips lifted, pressing his bulge against my inner thighs as he grew to meet my desire. I was ready for him to take me, but he stopped.

He pushed me away from him, and this time, he flipped me completely off his hard body, and I slid across the floor and slammed into the wooden leg of the large kitchen table. I groaned and whimpered. "What the fuck, Malachi? Why would you do that?"

"I told you. Control yourself." He got up from the floor and hesitated to get closer to me, as if he feared I would attack again. He reached for me and offered his hand. "I'm sorry. This isn't only a struggle for you. Sy, I am a male, and I am not exactly at the bottom of the food chain. My instincts took over. If I ask you to stop, stop. If you don't, I can and will make you stop, Sy. I am not like any human man. I can resist you if I want to."

"So, if I touch you, you toss me across the room. Got it." I got up from the floor and ignored his helping hand.

"Don't be that way." He sighed, frustrated as he tried to get me to understand. My ego was the one sporting the bruise this time around.

"What way is that exactly?" I turned away from him.

"Sore," he muttered. "I'm sorry, but this isn't that simple for me, either. Training a siren isn't exactly a part of the day job. They usually come with the knowledge of how to control themselves."

"Okay, I am not sore. My ass hurts, but I am not sore!" I walked over to the counter and sat down. If he wouldn't give me what I really wanted, I might as well eat. Malachi returned his own seat to an upright position and sat next to me. "I'm sorry," I whispered. I hated how he compared me to other sirens, and that I hadn't considered that there might be others in existence.

"Don't be." He watched me play with my food, still unable to summon an appetite.

"I don't know what has gotten into me. Last night I barely slept. Every time I closed my eyes, I was having sex dreams or reliving what happened..." I trailed off, remembering that I hadn't given him the details of my gym visit. After being rejected by him, that was the last thing I wanted to discuss.

"You're frustrated because you stopped before you finished your feed."

"Hmm," I stuffed my mouth full of eggs and refused to confirm or deny his allegation.

"Sy, I know what happened, even if you refuse to nut up and tell me all the details. I know where you were, and I know what you were doing."

I shoveled more eggs into my mouth. Perhaps if I kept eating, I would never have to confront this. My fork met the kitchen counter when he pulled the plate away from me. I looked up to meet his demanding expression.

"What do you want me to say?" I swallowed the eggs that were in my mouth.

"I want you to admit it to me," he said. "Tell me the truth about what happened."

"What good does that do, Malachi?" I reached for my juice, but he took it from me.

"Until you take responsibility for what is happening around you, things will only continue to worsen. I cannot help you if you refuse to help yourself." He spoke in a firm, yet even tone.

"Look, I came here because I want your help. I wouldn't be here if I didn't know I needed it. I know I am fucked up! Okay, I get that." I laid the fork on the counter and stared at my hand. "I'm no longer in control, and I hate it! Do you have to keep reminding me of that fact?" I stood from the counter and headed for the exit. Tears blurred my vision as I admitted for the first time aloud just how fucked up my life really was.

"Yes, I do!" he called to me.

"Why?" I turned to him.

"Because if I don't, you will break!" he challenged me, and I retreated. I couldn't face him.

"Whatever. I'm going back to my room." I stormed out of the kitchen and up the stairs. Before I made it to the third step, I felt him behind me.

He grabbed my right hip and spun me around. I lost my footing and fell back on the steps. My ass hit the step, and in the same moment, he pulled my shirt over my head. I could barely protest as he removed both my shorts and the panties I'd struggled to put on.

Eyes locked on mine, Malachi spread my legs and entered me. He didn't move; only filled me, reaching the base of my core and held there. He pulled my hair out of the sloppy bun I had put it in and wrapped my hair around his fist as his locs fell to cover my breast. I held my breath and focused on his eyes, which glowed a fiery red wrapped in ice blue like water illuminated.

"Don't resist it." He growled and bit down on my shoulder.

My body shook under his weight. The pressure of his form on top of me was crushing. There was no way I could ever resist him. I wanted him too badly. I squeezed my eyes shut. The feeling of him inside of me, not moving, but pulsating between my folds, was overwhelming.

My hands rested on his sides, and his muscles tensed beneath my palms as he held himself inside of me. I wanted him to move. I wanted the rhythm of his hips to feed my own. My hips shifted beneath him, lifting to his weight, and I hoped he would take the hint. I couldn't take his stillness much longer.

"What are you talking about?" I gasped as I felt him jump inside of me, hard against my walls.

"Let me in," he moaned, then kissed my neck.

"I don't know..." I couldn't finish my thought. "What do you mean?"

"Syrinada." He stopped. "Accept me fully. You want to feed from me, then feed, but you must welcome me inside of you, not just physically."

"I do." The soft moan slipped past my lips. "I want you."

He pulled back from me and then slammed into me again and again. My voice caught in my throat, and my stomach clutched. I bit my lip and threw my head back against the steps.

"Let it happen, baby," he whispered in my ear as he continued pushing me closer to my climax. "Don't hold back!" I opened my mouth to call out his name, but no sound came. "Damn it, Sy, stop resisting it! Let yourself go!"

He pulled away from me, flipped me on my stomach, and entered me again. I wanted to ask him what he was talking about, but my head was spinning. Confusion and ecstasy had taken over, and I was losing control.

His left arm wrapped around my waist, and his right hand clutched my throat. He slammed his body into me and held me tightly to him. His movement stopped again, and again, I was in agony as I waited for him to continue.

He didn't just pulsate inside of me; he moved his hips in small circles, adding a new rhythm to the motion. Hand still wrapped around my throat, he pulled my neck to him. My head rested on his shoulder, and his teeth grazed my neck. I couldn't take it; I couldn't let him tease me again.

I rocked my hips, moving myself in tight circles around him. I matched his pulsating by tightening my walls around him. His grip tightened, and he bit into my shoulder before he moved his hands to my hips. Again my internal grip tightened around him, and he lost the battle.

"Fuck," he groaned.

"Give it to me," I cried out and fell forward, lifting my ass in the air in front of him. I looked back over my shoulder just as he grabbed my hips and pulled me back to him.

"Yes!" I screamed and braced myself on the steps as he fucked me. *Finally!*

"Sy!" he said my name with such aggression. "Don't stop! Let me in!"

I looked back at him again, and when our eyes met, the surge of power pooled in my stomach. It started as a small bubble that expanded until it had nowhere else to go. I lifted from the steps, pushing back on his dick and sending him deeper inside of me.

"Come for me, baby," he bit into my shoulder.

The orgasm ripped through my body. When I opened my mouth to cry out, it wasn't my usual symphony of ecstasy. Instead, a sweet melody poured from within, and tears fell from my eyes.

CHAPTER II

I couldn't believe what just happened. Malachi had taken me. It was raw, and it felt amazing. I stood in the shower, finally able to find a point of calm. The water no longer aroused me but did what I needed and relaxed my body.

By the time I stepped from beneath the warm stream, it was all I could do to make it to the bed. I pulled the covers over my body and tucked myself away within the lingering warmth of the shower and the added heat of the bed. Then I was on fire again.

The returned dream of the underwater volcano and the glowing stone that called to me interrupted my peaceful rest. Once again, I made it to the top of the volcano, body burning. Just an arm's length away, and once again, I had failed. Completed the journey, only to fall into the mouth of the volcano as I reached for the stone.

When I opened my eyes, the soft glow of the moon filled the room. I yawned and stretched my arms above my head. For a moment I thought about normal things, like how I needed to figure out things for work, grocery shopping, and laundry. Seconds later, reality struck, and I realized that none of it mattered.

It didn't matter about work because at the rate things were going, I wouldn't be able to return, anyway. How would I explain it if I suddenly launched myself at the hot manager that I'd already been drooling over? He was a sexy Latin man with eyes the color of ash. Every time he looked at me, it was all I could do not to melt to the floor.

My siren side would chew him up and spit him out like a raisin. Then came the mental list of all the things I could no longer do and all the places it was no longer safe for me to go because I couldn't trust myself not to accidentally fuck a guy to death. *Tell me, how many girls had that problem to contend with?*

I heard movement in the house and got up, even though I felt like I could sleep for another couple of days. As if I hadn't just spent the entire day in bed. I pulled my gray sweats and hoodie out of the duffle bag, threw on my fuzzy socks, and headed down the stairs. I paused on the steps at the sound of laughter.

A man's voice, large and booming, but it wasn't Malachi. My heart slammed, and I froze in place because the voice and the scent of the man was already turning me on. My first thought was to retreat to my room, where I was safe from myself. I wasn't ready for this. I couldn't trust myself. How the hell was I ever supposed to operate in society again? I was turning into a fucking sex addict!

"Sy?" Malachi's voice reached me just as I turned to go back up the stairs. "Glad to see you're up and about."

"Uh, yeah. I figured it was about time to pull myself out of bed." I laughed half-heartedly, because at that moment, all I could think about was escaping the deep scent of the male that was still assaulting me.

"Good. Well, come on. I want you to meet someone." He chuckled, completely unaware of my internal struggle.

"Now?" We hadn't spoken about what happened. When it was over, we went our separate ways. Perhaps Malachi thought our encounter was enough to calm the seductress inside me. It clearly wasn't.

"Yes, is there a reason you can't?" Malachi stared at me and waited for my response. I could have told him the truth; that I felt moments away from jumping this mystery guest without even laying an eye on him. Instead, I sucked it up and prayed for the best.

"No reason, I guess." This was going to be bad. I followed Malachi to the large living room and tried quickly to avert my eyes. I gazed at the art and the high ceilings as if I had never seen them before. Perhaps if I never saw him, he couldn't have an actual effect on me.

"Sy, this is my brother, Demetrius. He just got home from a business trip to Morocco." Malachi spoke with an odd sense of pride as he made the introduction. *Could he possibly be that proud of his brother?* I shrugged the question aside and returned my focus to my breathing.

"Hello." Demetrius spoke to me, and I grabbed the back of the nearby chair. I needed something to hold on to as I struggled to bring my mind back to a functioning level. I could hear his steps carrying him across the room and feel the warmth of his body as he neared me. Eventually, I would have to look up at him and voice a response, but it didn't seem possible without attacking him.

My ass was already sore from Malachi tossing me across the room. He warned me to keep my control around these supposed alpha males. I didn't want to have to endure another injury or possibly die because I couldn't keep it in my pants.

"Sy? Are you okay?" Malachi thankfully made it back to me before his brother got too close and caused me to lose it.

"No, I'm not okay. I have got to get out of here." I looked at him, and that was all it took for him to understand. He ushered me out of the room, away from his brother.

Malachi made some excuse to his brother that I only partly heard. An apology for my not being able to face him. I directed all my brain power at keeping my body from turning to Demetrius. All I could do was refrain from inhaling anymore of his scent and move as quickly as possible back to the stairs.

When we made it to the room with the door securing me away from the scent of Demetrius, I allowed myself to breathe again. "That was insane. I'm so sorry."

"No, don't apologize. I should have known better." Malachi spoke, but disappointment replaced his previous swagger. I wasn't sure if his sudden display of was because of something I'd done wrong. It didn't seem like he was angry with me. That was an emotion I'd witness before, and it wasn't a calm display.

"Is this how it's going to be now?" I sat on the bed as I tried to catch my breath. "Anytime I am near a man, I will lose my shit?"

"No, but Demetrius is an alpha male, like I am. I should have known his presence would affect you. I guess I didn't consider the possibility that... and you are clearly in heat. But I just thought—" he trailed off and left the statement hanging in the air.

"I'm in heat? What the hell does that mean?" He spoke about me as if I was an animal. Dogs went into heat, not people!

"Seriously, do you need an explanation? You've been jumping men left and right," he snapped, and I backed down. There really was something to that alpha shit.

"Okay, so what now? I'm not allowed to be around any other man but you? And you never considered the possibility of what?" I posed my questions as calmly as I could. Malachi's temperature was rising, and to be honest, it frightened me, not that I would never admit that to him.

"No, well, I'm not exactly sure. Usually, when a female cries out her siren's call during sex, it means she bonded to her mate. You did that with me, and yet, Demetrius still affects you. I assumed you were the same, but maybe your mixed blood makes you different. The mated laws don't apply to you." Malachi spoke but wouldn't look at me. I could see his personal dilemma playing out on his face.

He was questioning himself. The oddities of my situation plagued his mind. Or was it his own uniqueness that troubled him? The part of himself he showed to me inside of my apartment. He lifted his hand to touch the necklace that hung against his chest. The question clearly written across his face. *Am I broken?*

Had his mother's transgression disfigured him in more ways than just his physical appearance? "Look, it doesn't matter." He opened the door. "Stay here. I'll talk to my brother and try to figure this out."

"I can always go home," I offered because I had nothing else to give. If my presence was making him doubt himself, the only way to resolve that was to remove me from the equation. Maybe there was someone else who could help me. Aunt Noreen would take me in.

"No, you can't. That much we already know." His statement was a sharp blow. I ignored it because I knew his tone was because my transgressions had hurt him. This wasn't the time to argue with him about it. "You need to be here. We just have to get a better understanding of our circumstances is all."

"Well, you can come with me," I offered another option. "You can teach me whatever it is I need to know at my place. I don't have to be alone there."

"I can't just abandon my home. We filled it with our family history and valuables. Someone has to be here to protect..." Again, he trailed off.

"Protect what exactly? Let me guess, that's something else you will have to clarify at a later date?" I asked, and he gave me a half smile before he left the room.

I could hear their voices beneath me. It was a brief conversation. Fifteen minutes later, Malachi returned alone.

"Demetrius will stay away until we can get you leveled out. Try to get some rest. We will start tomorrow," he spoke quickly and turned to leave.

"Start what exactly?" I couldn't let him go, but I couldn't bring myself to ask him to stay. It wasn't like I had any idea how to resolve any of the puzzles that were forming in his mind.

"Training you to be a siren... to be normal."

"Normal," I repeated. Was that even an option for me anymore? "Are you okay?"

"Yeah, I'm fine. Get some rest." He pulled the door shut and once again left me to myself.

I remained in my room for the rest of the night. Not because I was tired, but because I was afraid of the possibility of bumping into Demetrius before he had time to vacate the premises. I already upset Malachi enough. If he found me humping his brother... that would destroy him.

Instead, I took out my sketchpad and drew the images from my dreams. The way my stone sat teasingly at the mouth of

Ononolo, the lava that swallowed and dissolved my body, and the side of the volcano where bits of my flesh melted away from me. I couldn't get the images out of my mind fast enough. I sketched them repeatedly until my wrist burned from the motion.

Just as I had given up on sketching and moved to put the pad away, my stomach growled and reminded me I hadn't really eaten much in over a day. The couple of mouthfuls of eggs I scarfed down didn't count. I was still afraid of the consequences of leaving my room. When the hunger became too intense, I took my chances. Malachi's room wasn't far from my own. If I could make it to him, I should be safe to find out if his brother had left yet. If Demetrius were still there, I would just have to bug Malachi to get me some food.

I tapped on his door and waited. The longer it took him to answer, the more anxious I became. I heard sounds, someone talking, moving, and coming closer to me. My panic told me the best thing to do was hide. I quickly slipped through the door and pulled it closed quietly behind me. Malachi was lying on his bed, his snore the loud hum of a lawn mower. Like a creep, I just stood there and watched him.

There weren't many options for proceeding. On one hand, I needed to wake him up. I couldn't just stand there watching him like a perv, even though the image presented was an excellent one. I could walk over to him, try to tap him or shake him to wake him up, but nearing him seemed to be a highly dangerous idea. My body was already humming, completely thrumming with sexual energy just because I saw him like that. Apparently, that was all it took.

If I had gotten anywhere near him, I wouldn't be able to control myself. Malachi was right; I needed some serious help. Instead of approaching him, I tried to call his name softly. All that got me was a soft groan, which only worked to turn me on even more. I tried again, and he grumbled and flipped over, putting his ass into view. I bit my lip and held my breath for a moment. All I could think about was grabbing his firm ass as he thrust deep inside of me.

I took a step forward with every intention of doing something more than what I knew I should. Something that would probably get me hurt. Then I noticed a small ball on the dresser by the door, and I pulled back. I picked it up and aimed for the back of his head. Better to startle him from afar than to have him knock me across his bedroom. It landed harder than I thought it would have, smacking against his skull. Malachi flipped out of bed, poised and ready for a fight. I backed up into the dresser with my hands out in front of me, in a defensive position.

"It's just me, Sy! I'm sorry." I waved my hands in his face, hoping he recognized me before attacking. "I didn't mean to scare you."

"What the hell, Sy?" He stood up from his crouched position and rubbed the back of his skull, where the ball made contact. "Why would you do that?"

"I had to wake you somehow." I relaxed my stance once I realized he would not hit me.

"And smacking me in the back of my head was the only way you could think of?" He growled a bit, and I gripped the edge of the dresser, not because I was afraid but because it made something more primal stir inside of me.

"Yes, it was the only way that wouldn't get me tossed across the room for touching you when you didn't want to be touched." My eyes dragged across the length of his body, and he followed my gaze. He picked up a black T-shirt and quickly pulled it over his head. I thanked him with my eyes.

"What happened? Are you okay?" He looked closely at me and quickly assessed my condition.

"Nothing happened except I got hungry and wasn't sure if it was safe to walk the halls." I realized my tense stance wasn't helping to raise his opinion of me.

"Why wouldn't it be safe?" He wiped the sleep from his eyes.

"You know, two alpha males, one siren who is apparently in heat, a recipe for disaster as I understand it."

"Oh, right. Sorry. I should have let you know when D left. He is long gone. It's safe. Get whatever you need." He waved me off and sat back on the edge of the bed.

"Oh, okay. Thanks. I'm sorry for waking you. I'll go help myself."

"Sy." Malachi sighed and stopped me from leaving the room.

"Yes?" Okay, I admit it; I was excited that he didn't seem to want me to leave.

"Just now, you were... aroused by me?" His question caught me off guard.

"Yes... why? I'm sorry. That's why I didn't approach." I felt embarrassed with his eyes on me. He was assessing me again, but it wasn't to check if I was in good health.

"Hmm," was his only response.

"Is that all?" I spoke softly and hoped like hell that he would have more to say, that he would call me to his bed and take me. My insides flipped as I imagined our bodies tangled in his sheets.

"Yes. Sorry, go eat." He remained on the bed and watching him there aroused me again. Not that I had settled down to begin with. I bolted from the room. No, I wouldn't be getting any form of physical satisfaction. Great; the edible form would have to suffice for tonight.

I had just finished chomping down on my overloaded turkey sandwich when I noticed him. I felt him enter the room. It reminded me of being in the gym when the stranger arrived. My skin tingled, and my nostrils flared. His scent was so familiar to me now. It was all I wanted. I smiled to myself but erased it from my face before he could see it.

"You're still up?" I spoke without turning to him. I couldn't seem too eager to see him again, no matter what his presence did to me on a physical level.

"Yes, I couldn't seem to get back to sleep. Wonder why." I could hear him fiddling with the knife I had left on the counter.

"Would you like a sandwich?" I offered.

"No, I'm good." Malachi sat the seat across from me at the kitchen table. He just stared at me, didn't say a word, just watched as I ate and smiled at me.

"What is it?" It was making me uncomfortable. I hated to be stared at.

"What?" He chuckled because he knew exactly what I was referring to.

"Why are you looking at me like that?" I stopped eating and met his glare head on.

"Like what?"

"Goofy smile, staring… stop it, please." I held my hand up to block my face.

"Oh, sorry, it's just…" he trailed off; it was his way of teasing me. He always did it because he knew I couldn't leave it alone. I needed to know what he was going to say.

"It's just what?" I took a sip of juice and pushed my plate away. With my stomach full I looked him in the eye demanding a real explanation.

"Earlier, the incident with D, I thought maybe you had somehow become paired with him. It happens, that instant connection. Yet you still have physical responses to me, which wouldn't be there if you were paired with another alpha."

"So?" He had completely lost me.

"That doesn't happen, at least not naturally. Sirens can toy with human males all they want. Hell, to some of them it's a total game. They can use them up and toss them aside, no problem. However, with a male of our species, and an alpha male at that, it doesn't work that way. I assumed you and I were bonded because of your siren call, but that was incorrect, obviously." He wanted to look away. I could feel him getting ready to run, but I held his stare and dared him to face me.

"Well, you already said I was different. Maybe that's just another side effect of having my father's warlock blood running through my veins." I offered the idea to console him. I did not know what he was talking about or if warlock blood negated any of the siren in me. Malachi needed comfort, and that was all that mattered.

"I suppose that is a possibility." He bit his lip and thought hard about my words.

"And you're not actually happy about it, even though you were just sitting here and giving me that goofy smile."

"No, I am not." He sighed, "There is no way I could be happy about that, Sy."

"Why not?"

"Because it means all of this just got a lot more complicated than I had originally assumed it would be. Hell, it wasn't easy to begin with. You are so different already."

"You want me to be bonded to you." I swallowed hard because even if I didn't understand everything he was saying, the word *bonded* was heavily weighted in a commitment I wasn't sure I wanted. Everything about this was primal, and in primitive terms, to bond is forever.

"Yes, Sy, I do. That would make things so much easier."

"I don't see why anything would suddenly be easier. From my point of view, nothing about this has been easy." I pulled my plate back to me and bit into my sandwich to hide the frustration I felt because of his clinical response. I was still afraid to touch him. Malachi was still very much on edge; his male dominance had been threatened, and worse, by his own brother. I couldn't imagine what he was going through. He was one hundred percent correct. This would not be easy.

Chapter 12

Full-scale quarantine. Malachi had me on lockdown. My mentor kept his distance from me. He offered me books that covered our heritage to study through cracked doors. He even set up a meal schedule to avoid us bumping into each other in the hall. Each time I left the room, he was safely locked away. Good thing my bathroom was private and adjoined to my bedroom. I would have hated to have to inform him every time I needed to pee.

One minute I was perfectly fine, and then next, I felt like humping the damn bedpost. I was on a damn horn ball roller coaster. Being horny wasn't the only issue, as if that weren't problematic enough. Within a few nights, all kinds of freaky shit happened. Men would come banging down the door in the middle of the night in response to my siren's song, which Malachi told me I had sung in my sleep. This was a problem for more reasons than just the annoyance of the men who came continuously interrupting his sleep. He was afraid it would fall on the wrong ears and alert the witch covens of my existence.

That was just the beginning of the shit storm. Unexplained magical occurrences became a frequent complication. Yes, my father was supposedly a warlock, but knowing that did not prepare me to deal with shit bubbling up from that half of my bloodline, on top of trying to sort out the crap I inherited from my maternal parent. It was like I was some mythical time bomb, and the little clock had finally zeroed out.

When the mystical, magical shit happened, Malachi couldn't do anything to help me. The most he could offer me were looks of confusion and an old book about water spells he had found when he was a kid. He wasn't a warlock, and he couldn't begin to process things like levitation or items randomly combusting whenever I got upset, which was pretty often since he had cut me off from sex. He had no actual knowledge of witchcraft, and therefore, was a helpless bystander and the frequent target of my outbursts.

His frustration only added to my own. One week into our new routine, and I couldn't take it anymore. It was hard enough to feel out of control of my own body and actions, but it was so much worse to feel Malachi's agitation vibrating through the halls of the house and constantly assaulting me all damn day! It was like a dagger stabbing through me.

He tried to keep his disappointment from me. I gave him credit for that much, but it was like throwing a handkerchief over an elephant and then smacking that elephant on the ass, letting it run through the house while trying to look the other way. I had to get away, but I needed to wait until he was out of the house because there was no way he would allow me to just leave without supervision, or even at all.

During the second week, the others came. Men who apparently worked with Malachi and his brother. Not all were like us. They weren't sirens, but they were all supernatural in some way. The only ones I ever laid eyes on were the werewolves. Yes. Werewolves! That shouldn't have surprised me. Hell, if sirens and warlocks were real, anything was possible.

Demetrius sent these men to help his brother protect me. At least that was the way he explained it to me through a series of text messages. Honestly, I didn't feel protected; I felt like they were protecting others from me.

Malachi had left, gone to get groceries and to run a few other errands. I found this suspicious because he could have easily had one of the men do it, but maybe he needed to get away from our prison just as much as I did. That was my moment, my chance to escape. I needed time to clear my mind. I could leave for a bit and be back before he ever realized I was gone. He would never even have to know.

I hurried because I knew his lackeys would check on me. At that point, I had never laid eyes on them, but I knew they were there. They were all male and just as horny as I was. I was ready to claw down the walls and sniff their asses out. Not one of them was an alpha male on any level, so I found it easier to contain myself. Eyes were everywhere, but I tried to focus on not being seen. Malachi had already explained to me that when I wanted to be hidden, I could make it happen. After reading the material he gave me, I realized all I had to do was set my intention. So, I did.

First, I went into my bathroom because that was the only room in the house I hadn't sensed their presence. I turned on the shower to buy some time and provide noise to conceal my movements. I crept through the house, taking my time so I could avoid the stairs creaking under my weight as I descended them. It took longer than I would have liked, each second bringing Malachi closer to coming back to the house to notice my absence, but I finally made it out.

I made it to my car and away from the house with no incident and took that as a sign that my escape plan had worked. I rationalized my actions as I pulled away from the curb. All I needed was time to breathe. Was that so terrible? I needed to be away from all the insanity of what I was becoming and to pretend for just a little while that I wasn't already a monster. My first thought was to call Latasha. She'd been calling me, and besides a few texts to stop her from calling the police to report me as a missing person, we hadn't talked. I didn't know what I was supposed to tell her. Though I wanted to see my friend, I decided against it. That would be the first place Malachi would go looking for me. Instead, I drove the car straight into the city.

It was early on a Friday night, a busy time in the streets of downtown Chicago, even in the winter. People wanted to play, no matter how frigid the temperatures. The party goers were coming out to fill the streets, while the laborers headed home from a long day of work. I parked in a lot and paid no fee as the attendant all but fell into the car when I cracked the window to hand him the twenty dollars. I smiled at him; he handed me a ticket and waved me on.

I exited on the opposite side of the lot when I got out of the car because I didn't want to have to deal with his advances. I didn't find him to be particularly attractive. Therefore, there seemed to be no risk of me jumping his bones, but there was no telling what he might try to do. Obviously, I had reached a point in my life where men were automatically not worthy of my trust. Kidnapping and attempted rape had that effect on a girl.

Walking down the street was an entirely new experience. Men lingered and stared at me hungrily. Women, well... if looks could kill... you know the expression. I remembered Latasha telling me before this was what she witnessed whenever she was out with me, but I never believed her. Now that my eyes were open to the truth, it was hard not to notice the reaction other people had toward me. It would also explain why I had almost no female friends.

I tried not to focus too much on the women I passed. They would never approach me anyway, and if they did, I was sure I could handle myself. I found myself just a few blocks from the Willis Tower (I use the current name, but it will always be Sears Tower to me! I didn't care who bought the damn building.) Right at the corner of Jackson and Clinton, I stopped, because my stomach growled, and the smell of Beggars Pizza beckoned me.

The chairs and tables were set up for curbside dining, and the food smelled delicious. Inside, the restaurant was packed, and it overloaded my senses. After grabbing a large slice and a Coke, I sat outside in the crisp January air and ate because I didn't trust myself to stay inside the crowded establishment. I had the outside to myself because I was the only one brave enough to risk the icy Chicago Hawk blowing through and smacking me in the head.

I finished my slice quickly to avoid it getting cold and was sipping on my Coke when a very handsome guy walked by. Okay, he wasn't just handsome; he was fucking yummy! He was tall; strong build. His peat coat hung open to reveal a gray suit with a blue tie that matched his eyes. He had short dirty blonde hair and a smile that belonged on the cover of a magazine. He flashed that smile and waved at his buddy as they reached the corner and went their separate ways. I watched as he walked by. My only thought was I wanted him to look at me. He did, of course, but he kept walking.

After he looked at me, there was only one thought I could process. Whoever this guy was, I wanted him. I stood from my seat and maneuvered my way through the tables, making it to the sidewalk so I could follow him. He kept a steady pace as he walked down the street and into a parking garage. I hopped in the elevator with him, and we rode to the top floor. I was sure his car was not there; it was just prime real estate for two people with a mutual unspoken agenda. No one would be up there. The place was all but deserted, with just a few old cars, which probably belonged to the staff. There was not one car here I could remotely picture this Armani suit wearing man driving.

The elevator doors closed, and the little bell sounded as he turned to me and smiled, and I was on him in a hot second. Now, let me take the time to say I was not intending to be reckless. I had studied this intently. It was the first thing I looked up when Malachi gave me all that reading material. It seemed to be the only thing that really mattered, considering all the bad things I had already done. I had to know I could be with a human man, enjoy him, and not harm him.

The key was to be in control of my emotions and to remain levelheaded. As long as nothing pissed me off, and as long as I remained focused, no harm should come to him. I just wanted to be pleased, to feel his body, and enjoy the hidden pleasures of this man. It was warm for the end of January, but still cold. Not that it mattered; I pulled his clothing from him quickly and bit into his shoulder. He moaned aloud as I worked my way across his body.

A small, appreciative moan slipped through my lips as I undressed him. This man was like a sculpture, completely chiseled. He had the abs of a bodybuilder, but he was lean like a swimmer.

I reminded myself of my intentions as he tore open my jacket and popped the buttons off my shirt. I kept my mind trained as he pulled out my breast and hungrily kissed and nibbled on my nipples. I remained in control as I pulled his warm length from his pants. I was even in control as he bent me over the hood of the small blue car and entered me from behind. I felt so damn amazing, and for the first time since I dropped my cell phone the night I was taken, I felt truly in control. I didn't hurt him; he didn't burst into flames or shrivel up and wither away. When I left him, he was half-naked, leaning against an SUV, and panting like a little puppy. When I left him, he was fine. *Then I blinked.*

I blinked, and I was standing above a body, one that was in no sense of the word, fine. It was hollowed and empty, a gray husk. My vision blurred, and I tried to straighten out the jumble of details that moved around in broken patterns inside my mind. Everything felt oddly glazed over by the lingering ecstasy of the parking garage treat. I couldn't remember what happened or why I was standing over this crust that clearly used to be a man. I was panting and sweating as the world around me slid into a sensible configuration, so I could see again. The recollection of my actions came in a slow wave, driving across town and hunting this man down.

He was a part of that gang, those assholes who hurt me. He had inherited the title as leader of the pack once the old king's head exploded. I looked at his apartment. It was nice, much nicer than the predecessor's place. Perhaps he was better at what he did; ran the business in a more lucrative manner. Good for him, the sick fuck!

I walked around the apartment, and yes, it was an actual apartment. Two bedrooms. One was his own, with the feminine touches that told me he wasn't single. When I entered the second room, I puked. The room belonged to a little girl. Princesses and Barbie dolls stared out at me from every corner. This sick asshole was the father of a little girl. The same guy, who had it not been for his disgusting leader, would have happily accepted the opportunity to rape and murder me! *He was a fucking father!* I fell to my knees and screamed.

The emotions I felt were overwhelming. On one hand, it satisfied me that the sick fuck was dead, but on the other hand, there was a little girl who would now have to live her life without a father. That was a familiar pain. I knew what it felt like to wonder what you did to deserve something that was entirely out of your control. I sat on the floor of the little girl's bedroom much longer than I should have and was there so long that the police arrived, and I had to hide myself again to prevent them from seeing me. Officers moved around my hidden presence as they investigated the scene. Apparently, one of his neighbors saw his body on the floor through his window when he returned from work.

When I finally picked myself up, I left through the back stairs. I couldn't risk the elevator, because though it would have been faster, it just wasn't safe. There would be no way to avoid it if someone got in with me and wondered why there was an invisible barrier between them and the wall. As I descended each flight, the level of my panic increased. I felt the internal pressure as it built. I was a murderer; it didn't matter how I tried to justify my actions; the title was mine to claim.

It was easy to wipe out the men who hurt me, as long as I didn't think about the people who loved those men. The families who would miss them once they were no longer around to pick up helpless girls from the street and have their way with them. I exited the building behind a fat cop, the same one that had been in the hospital, more interested in his donut than finding the asshole that hurt me. *Fucker.*

Reaching the corner of the street, I stopped walking as I realized I did not know where my car was. I stood there scratching my head like a moron. My stomach felt like it was going to turn inside out. I placed my hand across my midsection and rubbed my stomach in small circles to help calm the internal rage. The last thing I wanted was to vomit again.

"What the hell did you do? What happened in there? How could you be so reckless?!" Malachi barked out his questions in hushed frustration as he pulled me into the shadows with him. "I can't believe you! Do you have any idea what you have done?"

"Look, I feel shitty enough as it is! I don't need you in my face right now!" I pushed away from him and headed back to the curb to continue my confused search for my car. I wasn't surprised to see him there. I was more concerned that he hadn't arrived sooner.

"Syrinada, you are going to have to deal with a lot more than me getting in your face!" He grabbed me by the shoulders and spun me around to face the street behind me just as the news trucks pulled up. "Do you have any idea what you have done? Do you see this shit? The media will be all over us, and because of your little hideaway act, I couldn't get here in time to clean up your shit! It's not just you, Sy! We are all in danger of being found now!" Malachi stared at me, bore into me with his gaze until his words hit home and the sick feeling returned.

He had explained to me about the hidden community of our people that existed in and around Chicago. There were full families of siren descendants that were blended into human society.

His eyes told me that what I had done would call attention to not only me, but to all of them. I had selfishly brought danger upon all of them, and I couldn't even remember making the decision to do so.

What followed was a blur. I moved as I was instructed, but something detached me from my body. I felt ashamed. My guilt formed around Malachi's words. He couldn't get there in time to clean up my shit. I had become exactly the kind of woman my aunt had told me about. Reckless, doing only what pleased me, regardless of how my actions affected anyone else. Add to the list that there were now entire families who would suffer because of me. I had never been that way before, the type to be so selfish or heartless. Because I was stir crazy, I had put myself above them all. I was losing myself. I was losing sight of who I was.

As the world moved around me, he pelted me with questions I had no answers for. My mind formed them back to back, an assembly line of painful shocks of reality. Each one was worse than the last. I pushed them all to the side, but there was one topic I couldn't turn away from. It ate away at me. *Was that the reason the stone called to me? Was it the reason behind the dream?* Only the worst sirens, the evil ones, ever cared to chase down their stones. What if I was one of them?

CHAPTER 13

We made it back to the house with Malachi behind the wheel of my car, which we found five blocks away from the apartment complex. I sat in the living room of his home and watched him as he anxiously paced the room and tried to decide what to do. He clutched his cell phone in his hand so tightly that his knuckles lost their color. His muttered ramblings were a debate of whether he should call Demetrius. He wasn't sure if that was the move to make, considering that my condition was still so uncontrolled.

"Are you going to call him?" A brute of a man spoke from the corner. He'd been watching me like a hawk from the moment we returned to the house. He, like the rest of the males who had conveniently come out of hiding, didn't trust me not to make a run for it.

Maurice was tall, dark-skinned, and fit, but as imposing as his form was, he had the sad stench of a beta male. He was simply secondary. Compared to Malachi, Maurice was unimpressive, and the thought of him touching my body turned my stomach. As much as it sickened me, I inhaled more of his scent because it helped to deter my arousal as I watched Malachi's muscular legs carry him back and forth across the floor in front of me.

Even though logic told me I was wrong, I would have sworn he was trying to tease me when he stopped and wrapped his hands around his dreads that were pulled back into a low pony-tail. He released them from the holder and allowed them to fall down around his shoulders. I took a big whiff of Maurice and held it in as long as I could.

"I don't know. I probably should, but is it worth the risk? We have no proof that this has actually compromised us." Malachi looked conflicted, as if he couldn't bring himself to believe his own words.

"We don't yet, but you know damn well that the covens will investigate what happened back there and that will lead them right to us. That shit is already all over the news! How long do you think it will take them to connect the dots?" Maurice was upset, but he seemed to me to be overly aggressive about the situation.

He looked like he was ready to go to war. Everyone was on edge, but there was something about him in particular that was just completely over the top. I wasn't sure about my intuition, but he actually looked guilty, like there was something he was hiding from Malachi.

What could he have to feel guilty about? I was the one who had fucked up. Maybe he knew I had left and chose not to say anything about it. Regardless of what it was, he needed to chill out. I watched him as he moved a step closer to Malachi, and I felt myself bristle.

I didn't trust his ass, and something in me wanted to protect Malachi from him. He noticed it, but Malachi didn't seem to. Maurice stepped back, and for a moment held my gaze, as if searching for something. He looked at Malachi and back to me, and I could have sworn I saw fear in his eyes. No wonder he wasn't the leader. How could he be if he were afraid of me?

"Look, I hear you, okay? But this is different." Malachi looked at me, then back to the beta. "Man, she is different! I have to make sure whatever I do is right for everyone!"

"Somehow I don't think you have what's right for everyone in mind." Maurice huffed.

"Excuse me?" Malachi challenged his blatant accusation of Malachi's authority.

"Come on, man. All this shit we've been going through, and for what? To protect this bitch?"

"Excuse me?" I snapped at his outburst, and Malachi placed his hand on my shoulder. He squeezed it gently to let me know he would defend me, and I didn't need to get upset.

"Watch your mouth, Maurice," Malachi warned him.

"Are you serious right now?" Maurice took another step back, placing himself closer to the exit. "What the hell is this, man? I thought we were family!"

"We are family, and family respects boundaries. You're crossing one right now." This time the low, throaty rumble came from Malachi. An audible warning for Maurice to back down.

"You know what, Malachi? You can take your shit somewhere else. I am not uprooting my family again for this b—" Maurice wasn't able to finish his statement before Malachi was on him. He had warned him, and yet Maurice challenged his authority again. Malachi picked the man up by his throat and carried him across the room, where he slammed his back against the wall.

"Say it again. I dare you!" Malachi growled at the scared male. He tightened his grip, and Maurice whimpered.

"This is fucked up, man, and you know it is." Maurice choked as he clutched Malachi's hand, not able to free himself from the hold. It barely looked as if Malachi was exerting any force, and yet Maurice was clearly struggling to remain conscious.

"That is your opinion, one I don't recall asking you for. Back down, Maurice, or this will not end on good terms." Malachi's fist landed hard against the wall, inches away from Maurice's head.

"Fine, do whatever you want. However, trust me when I say, I am not putting the lives of my family on the line for her! She is just like the rest of her bloodline. Nothing but death will follow that girl!" He looked over Malachi's shoulder and stared at me, adding emphasis to his statement.

"Get out, Maurice, and don't come back." Malachi growled at him and released his hand from around his throat.

Maurice fell to the floor and hurried to run away. Before he left the room, he looked over his shoulder at me, and I couldn't help it; I allowed the growl to roll up my throat in response. That was going to take some time to get used to, the involuntary responses I was having to my surroundings. Growls, heightened senses of sight, touch, and smell; I felt like an animal, more primal than before.

"What was that about?" I asked as Malachi returned to my side.

"That was about us leaving." His shoulders slumped forward as he sat down next to me.

"What, leave and go where?" I spoke softly and tried not to agitate him. This was a difficult situation already without my questioning. Because of me, he had already pushed his brother away, and now his own people were turning against him. I understood the sensitivity of it all, but I had questions and needed answers.

"Away from here. We can't stay. What that idiot said wasn't completely false. The witch covens will come here looking for answers. They're going to want to know who killed that man, and it won't take them long to figure out it was a siren. They might now know about you yet, but either way, we can't afford to take the risk that they come here and find out. If they find you, they will kill you and anyone near you. I cannot risk your life or the lives of everyone here." He pulled out his cell phone again and flipped it around in his hand. "The best we can hope is that they think whoever the culprit is, is already on the move and they won't mess with anyone else here."

"And where are we going, Malachi?"

"I have to call my brother. I need him to come back." He shook his head, as if already regretting what he was about to do.

"Demetrius? But isn't that a bad idea... considering..." I dropped my eyes to my hands and kept the rest of my thought to myself.

"Considering what? Considering that you refuse to listen to me? Alternatively, that you have become so reckless with your life and the lives of everyone around you? I have no other choice right now." He sighed and ran his hand down his face. "We have to go, and he is the only one I trust to help us right now. As you can tell, you aren't exactly a fan favorite in this community."

"Yeah, I got that much from Maurice, thanks. Do you really think it's a good idea to bring in Demetrius? I mean, can't we handle this on our own? Do we really need him in order to move?"

"Where we need to go, unfortunately, he needs to be with us. Demetrius is older than I am and more experienced in certain areas. We will need his experience and connections on our side." Malachi tapped the screen of his phone and brought up his brother's profile. I averted my eyes from the soulful smile that was displayed on the screen.

"Where are we going exactly?" I repeated my previous question.

"New Orleans, to the swamps where the seers are."

"Seers?" I hadn't read up on them yet, but one of the books he'd given me mentioned their existence.

"Yes, they were next up on your history plan, followed by the pixies and unicorns." He shook his head, and his hair fell around his face as he laughed. "Ironic, isn't it? Damn lesson plan."

"I don't think I will ever get used to this stuff."

"You will in time." Malachi got up from the couch to walk away from me so he could have privacy when he made the call he didn't want to make.

"Malachi, I am sorry. I really am," I admitted to his back.

"Yeah, I know. It's just... I hate to say this to you, but I am getting tired of hearing you apologize." He spoke with his back to me, but I could hear the total disappointment in his voice.

"That's harsh." I dropped my head.

"Maybe, but maybe it's what you need right now. I tried to be nice about it. Each time you ignored my warnings." The strain of his voice caused me to feel shame, genuine regret for everything I had done to disrupt his life.

"I said..." I started.

"Yeah, I know. You are sorry. Funny how that changes nothing at all." Malachi walked away and left me to sit under the weight of his words, and they were crushing what little life I had left out of me.

I waited in my room after Demetrius arrived, because Malachi wanted to brief Demetrius on the situation without me. He said it would make it easier without the added concern of what I would do. It wasn't difficult to tell that the situation made him unhappy. He didn't want Demetrius around me, especially knowing I had an attraction to him. I told him I could control myself, but neither of us believed that. So, he sent me to my room to wait until he came to get me. He said he would come for me himself and escort me down. I felt like a psych patient. *Must contain the crazy.*

"Sy?" Malachi opened the door and peeked in on me. "You ready?"

"Yes, I guess I am. As ready as I will ever be for this." I stood from the bed. "So, how are we doing this?"

"Just come on. We will walk in, and if you feel at all unstable or as if you will do anything at all, like you cannot control your actions, let me know, and I will get you out of there."

"And if I can't, what happens then? I mean, you said we need him to come with us, right? How does any of this work if we can't even be in the same room together?"

"We will figure it out. Let's cross that bridge if we come to it, okay?" He pushed the door further open so I could exit.

"Okay, lead the way." I stepped to the side to let him take the lead down the hallway.

I followed Malachi down the stairs and into the living room, where Demetrius stood with his back to us. He was as still as a statue, a part of Malachi's cautionary plan. Demetrius stared out the window, and I watched him as closely as I could, while I made my approach. I was attentive to my breathing and scrutinized my reaction to him. Strong back lines covered in tight jeans beneath a worn leather jacket. I watched his muscles contract and release with each breath and the side of his jawline, which tightened as he sensed me nearing him. My arousal was near instant, and the smell of my excitement filled the air.

I glanced at Malachi, and his expression pained me. I wanted to apologize, but for what? My body was having a chemical reaction, one that was completely out of my control. What I could control was my actions. Just because my body responded to him didn't mean anything more had to happen. I reached out, grabbed Malachi's hand, and clutched it tightly. He looked down at me and gave me a weak smile. He knew I would never intentionally do anything to hurt him. I swallowed the knot in my stomach, nodded, and signaled to him it was okay to continue.

"Demetrius, this is Sy," Malachi announced, not looking away from me.

I pulled my eyes from him to see his brother as he turned around to face us. My eyes swept across his broad shoulders, up his throat, noting the movement of his Adam's apple as he swallowed and continued across his shadow-dusted jaw. I took in his full lips, hazel eyes, and his locs that matched Malachi's. I swallowed hard and pulled my fingers even tighter around Malachi's hand. In hindsight, that may have been the wrong thing to do, as it gave Malachi confirmation of his fears.

"Hello, Syrinada," Demetrius spoke, and all knowledge of the processes of breathing escaped my brain. The sound of my name from his mouth was musical, maddening, enticing, and sexual. I wanted to reach out and grab him, pull him into me, and spend hours with him inside of me. Instead, I took a deep breath, concentrated only on the scent of Malachi, and I forced my brain to compose semi-coherent thoughts.

"Nice to meet you." I stuck my free hand out to shake his. He grabbed it, lifted it palm up to his lips, and kissed my skin before turning my hand over to leave the hot impression of his lips there as well. Malachi bristled beside me, and Demetrius dropped my hand and looked at his brother remorsefully. "I apologize. I have lost my manners."

"Yeah, just keep it in check, okay?" I didn't like the way Malachi responded. This situation wasn't exactly easy for any of us. We were all trying hard to avoid a catastrophe.

"Easy there, little brother." Demetrius chuckled and pushed his locs back over his shoulder. "It seems we have something of a problem here, and we will have to work together to solve it. As you thought, the covens are aware of what happened here, and we must move. My sources tell me they will send their minions to investigate the events as soon as the humans leave the scene of the crime. Our leaving this place is the only way to ensure our people who are still in the area remain safe. They won't lift a finger against an innocent soul, but I know they will come for us. They will track Syrinada much easier considering that, in some sense, she is one of their own."

"So, how do you suggest we transport?" Malachi had calmed enough to speak without clutching his jaw.

"Road trip. They own the airways, no way to slip through unnoticed."

"Is that really safe? And to drive to New Orleans from Chicago, that would take a long time," I questioned and looked at Malachi because it was easier. He was my friend above anything else, and he brought my mind back to a level state.

"Yes, but unfortunately, it is the only option we have if we don't want to risk being caught by them," Demetrius answered my question. "I suggest we get on the road first thing in the morning, before sunrise."

"I agree; it's risky to still be here, even now." Malachi turned to face me. "Let's go. We can visit your apartment and give you a chance to gather anything you will need. I can't say how long it will be until we get back. Anything of importance to you, take now."

"Oh okay. What about Latasha?" I asked. I hadn't spoken to my friend, but I knew she was waiting for the tea.

"Who?" his brother questioned as we walked away. I stopped and looked over my shoulder to answer him.

"My friend. She will more than likely be there waiting since I haven't been home in a while, and she will have questions. What am I supposed to tell her?" I looked from him to Malachi because he knew Latasha and would have the same level of concern for her as I had. Demetrius was the one to bring a resolution to my concerns.

"Oh, right. The loud one. Well, you tell her the truth; that things have gotten complicated here and you need to get away for a while to sort it out. There's no sense in lying. Just leave out any of the witchy details. Give her the chance to survive this. If the witches find her, they will question her and see that she knows nothing, so they will leave her alone," Demetrius spoke. "I will make sure someone monitors her." He smiled at me, and I could feel my cheeks warm and begged them not to, for Malachi's sake.

"Let's go." Malachi huffed.

My face had apparently ignored my wish, considering the way Malachi stormed out of the room. I ran to grab my jacket and followed him out the door. I couldn't help myself. I glanced over my shoulder at Demetrius one more time; he was standing there watching me. He smiled at me, and I felt my pulse quicken. Yeah, this was going to be one fucked up road trip.

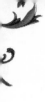

CHAPTER 14

When we got to my apartment, Malachi told me to hold back while he went up ahead of me to see if Latasha was around. If she were, he would try to get her into her apartment and keep her distracted while I grabbed my things. I didn't see his plan failing, considering she was no doubt still itching to get dirt on us. Especially since his impromptu announcement of a sexual encounter was immediately followed by both of us falling off the face of the Earth. I was sure she'd concocted more than a handful of theories about how all the pieces fit together in that scandalous puzzle.

"She isn't here." Malachi stuck his head through the door and called down the stairwell, where I waited for confirmation to proceed.

"Good." That was a relief because what his brother said made sense. I didn't want to lie to Latasha, but the less she knew about everything, the better it was for her.

"Yeah, come on. Let's get this done before Latasha shows up."

In my apartment, Malachi stood watch next to the door while I moved around and tried to decide what items were important enough for me to be concerned about taking with me. The idea of never returning to this place no longer upset me as much as it did before. I felt detached from it and all the material possessions it contained.

"Are we going to discuss this?" I gave up on my search for items of importance and returned to Malachi.

"Discuss what?" He leaned away from the door with a confused expression.

"Us, whatever is going on between us, and now your brother? His being back changes things. I don't know how or why, but I can sense the change, and I know you can as well, Malachi." I dropped the bag I'd been filling on the floor. "So, are we going to discuss it or not? Because I feel like we should talk about all of it. And it's probably best to do it here, before we get back to the house where Demetrius can hear us."

"I don't know what to say to you." He leaned his back against the wall next to the door and waited for me to continue.

"Look, I know that this is hard for you. Maybe I can't fully understand how all of this really affects you, but I am trying to keep things in perspective."

"You're right. This is hard for me, and it is very unlikely that you can truly understand it." He stepped away from the wall and came closer to me. "I don't enjoy feeling that I want to rip out my own brother's throat. But I also don't like what obviously exists between the two of you."

"Okay, I get that but—"

"Do you?" Malachi paced in front of me and ran his hands through his dreads. "Do you get how sick I feel when he looks at you or how it kills me to feel your body reacting to him in ways it should only respond to me? Do you know how much I hate the sound of your name as it passes his lips or that you blush like a damn schoolgirl whenever he says it?" He took another step closer to me.

"I'm sorry," I apologized, even though I had no fault in my primal responses.

"Stop saying that. Apologizing doesn't fix what's broken, Sy, it only makes this worse."

"Seriously?" I bristled at his words.

"Look, I'm not trying to sound so insensitive. All I mean to say is that you don't have to keep apologizing to me." His last step brought his body against my own as he wrapped his arms around me.

"Well, what do you want me to say?" I looked up at him and wished I could remove the sadness from both his eyes and my heart. We were both hurting, but for completely different reasons, and there were no solutions in sight.

"There is nothing you can say, and I am not asking for you to say anything at all. Words won't fix any of this. We're in a fucked up situation right now. There is nothing we can do about it except get away from here, so we can take time to regroup and figure out our next step."

"Yeah, it is pretty fucked up. I will admit that, but how are we supposed to handle it? A road trip with the three of us sounds like a total disaster. You've already admitted that you want to cause him bodily harm. Do you think you can handle a long drive like that together without attacking him? I seriously don't want the two of you to come to blows over me."

"Look, this will be hard, but I can handle myself. I am not a monster, even though lately I've felt like one. D is my brother, and we will work together to protect you, as we always have." He lowered his lips to place a soft kiss on my forehead.

"That still makes me feel uncomfortable. The thought that you've known all about me for so long and you said nothing to me about any of it." I pulled back from him, and he dropped his arms from around me. "Why didn't you just tell me? Why not avoid all of this?"

"It wasn't my place to interfere. To be honest, I had hoped I would never have to. I knew this transition would be hard on you. No, I wasn't expecting all the current complications, but I knew it wouldn't be easy for you. Especially coming into it now, having two supernatural groups who are after you because of who your parents were." Malachi remained at ease as he explained. "As I said before, the chips are stacked against you. They marked you as a threat without ever taking the time to get to know you or to be sure that their assumptions about you were correct. The longer you remained unaware of this world, and of this part of yourself, the longer you remained safe. That was all that mattered to me, keeping you safe."

"I see." I stepped back into his waiting arms and lifted onto my toes to kiss him. What he said to me was exactly what I needed to hear. They were the words I was waiting for without realizing it. He hadn't kept this all from me because he knew I would be a monster, or because he was afraid I would ruin his life. He did it all for me; to protect me. He became a part of my world, yet he never wanted to interrupt it. I thought about the first time I saw him, that unexplained excitement I saw in his eyes, and my lips curled into a smile against his.

"There is something that bothers me. Something I can't figure out," he said as our kiss ended, and my stomach knotted because I knew whatever was going to follow wouldn't be good.

"What's that?" I gave him one more peck on the lips before our bodies parted.

"That night they attacked you. It just doesn't make sense to me."

"Why not? Drug addicts do awful stuff all the time." I retrieved the one bag I had that contained mostly items for personal hygiene. Who knew if they would have my brand of shampoo where we were going? *I mean, they don't sell Suave everywhere!*

"Yes, that much is true, but we've had you under surveillance, Sy. Your absence went unnoticed. When I asked my men about it, they seemed completely clueless about the whole thing. I checked, and they reported nothing that reads even remotely questionable about that night."

"So, what are you saying?" I shut off the lights and double-checked the place.

"I'm saying it doesn't add up, and that I am seriously questioning some of my alliances right now." He waited by the door, still listening to see if he could hear Latasha approaching. His men were watching the outside of the building and were supposed to notify us if she arrived, but he clearly didn't trust them to do their job.

"You think someone set me up?" I asked.

"Unfortunately, yes. I believe you may have been, but I can't figure out by who or how. Who would profit from your being hurt?"

"That's fucked up." I sat on my bed and thought about the implications. "It also means we have a lot more to worry about than my hormone levels peaking at the wrong time. If someone set me up, it means they wanted me dead and are currently really pissed that I'm not, or they intended to trigger this shit. If this is what they wanted, well, why?"

"Exactly, who would benefit from your disappearance? That's the question I can't seem to answer." He pulled the door open slightly and stuck his head out. Not finding anyone in the hall, he turned back to me. "Do you have everything?"

"I guess. I mean, I am not even sure what I am supposed to be taking with me. What use is any of this stuff?"

"It's good to have things around you that remind you of home and of better times, especially considering how majorly screwed up this is all turning out to be."

"Right, and having my favorite sweater with me will make all of that so much better?" I laughed.

"No, but it is something that may make it easier to handle." He looked around. "Trust me, you don't want to lose everything. Demetrius and I have spent so many years just trying to track down items that were lost to us. They matter."

"Yeah, okay. Let's go. I can't think in here, and it's just really hitting me that nothing here is all that important to me." I looked around the room. "There is nothing here I couldn't see my life without."

"Nothing at all?" Malachi seemed worried by the sentiment.

"No, unfortunately. I guess I never became attached to anything." I scanned my home again and shook my head when again I came up with nothing that mattered. "What do you think that says about me?"

"I don't think it says anything."

"Right." He was lying, but I would ignore it. I had enough personal revelations; I didn't need to add anything else to that list.

Latasha never came home. I knew it was for the best, but I wanted to see her again. To say goodbye and let her know not to worry about me. Instead, as we drove away from our apartment complex, I sent her a text message.

Sy: *Hey, stopped by the building. Sorry I missed you.*

Tasha: *Stopped by, as in you're going to be gone again? Where have you been?*

Sy: *Just handling some stuff with my family.*

Tasha: *Family? Your aunt? Is she okay?*

Sy: *Yes, she is fine. I'm going to be going out of town for a while. Just wanted to let you know I'm okay and not to worry.*

Tasha: *Is this trip with Malachi?*

I didn't respond. I couldn't lie to her, and I couldn't confirm it either. Like Demetrius said, the less she knew, the better.

When we made it back to his house, I rushed from the car to my room, avoiding any contact with the men of the house. The bed was the safest place for me. I sat alone in the dark with the only thing that mattered in my life, the picture of my mom. The emotions I had been holding in exploded from me in sobs. I could no longer be brave or strong, not even for myself.

I cried and wished she were here to hold me and tell me that everything would be okay. This was the same wish I'd made almost every night since I was a little girl and one I would probably continue to make for the rest of my life. It wasn't fair that she lost her entire life just for loving a man and having a child. It would never stop hurting. I would never forgive myself for being the reason for my own mother's death.

The next morning, before the sun had time to light the sky, Malachi tapped gently on my door. After a sleepless night, I was wide awake and itching to get out of the room. When he poked his head in through the crack, I looked up to him from the edge of the bed where I sat, completely dressed, and clutching my phone in my hand.

"You ready to go?" He pushed the door further open. "We are all packed up. I just need to load your stuff."

"Yeah, I guess so." I pointed to my bags, which were packed and sitting in the middle of the floor.

"It doesn't look like you slept very well."

"Yeah, no. I didn't sleep at all. My brain was in overdrive all night." I looked at him, and my vision blurred from the motion of turning my head.

"Well, you can catch some sleep in the car." He smiled, mocking my obvious discomfort. "You'll be like a baby, you know, the second the motor starts, they pass right out."

"Yay. Did you know that lack of sleep gets painful?" I said dryly. I moved to pick up my bags from the floor, and Malachi laughed. "And what exactly is so funny?"

"You are. You look like a damn zombie." He chuckled. "Just, go get in the car. I will bring down your stuff. Is everything here in the bags?"

"Yes." I wanted to retort, to have some great comeback, but I was just too tired to care. Malachi was right. I didn't think I would make it ten minutes once the car got moving.

"Are you sure you can make it on your own?" He laughed, and I stuck my tongue out at him in response.

I climbed down the stairs carefully and clutched the banister, hoping to avoid falling on my face. The last thing I needed was to give Malachi more fuel for his mockery. I could just imagine the huge laugh it would get if they found me face planted on the first floor. Odds were, I wouldn't have the strength to recover before one of them found me.

"You okay?" Demetrius' voice came from behind me just a moment before he grabbed my forearm to help me down the last of the steps.

"Um... Yeah. I'm just tired. Had a hard time sleeping last night." I pulled my arm from his hold as we made it to the bottom of the steps. "I'm good, thank you."

"Sure, no problem." Demetrius caught my gaze and held it. His intense expression was one of understanding. I set a boundary, and he respected it.

A simple head nod was all I could muster with my tired mind. A tired mind apparently also meant that my body was too tired for a physical response. I stood there for a moment after he left to be sure I'd be able to walk again, and then ambled across the hall and out the door, never stepping too far away from the wall, just in case. The oversized backseat of the black SUV was a fortunate discovery. It meant plenty of space for my tired body to relax in. It took a minute, but I found a comfortable position curled up into the leather and waited for the guys to join me.

A few minutes after I settled in, the two brothers emerged from the house, laughing about zombies. They were clearly talking about me, and had I had more energy, I might have said something about it. I committed each of their smart comments to memory. Each one a little grudge I would use as fuel for later jabs of my own. I looked up at Malachi, who glanced over his shoulder from the passenger seat at me. He smiled with a quick wink just as my eyes slid shut.

When I opened my eyes, the car was sitting at a gas station. A glance at the camera on the dashboard informed me we'd been on the road for about five hours. I couldn't believe I had slept for so long or that I felt so rested. Usually sleeping in a car did more to add discomfort, back pain, and a serious crook in my neck, but I felt rejuvenated. Demetrius sat in the passenger seat, replacing Malachi, who was there when I closed my eyes. When I glanced at the driver's seat, it was empty.

"Where are we?" I stretched my arms and sat up.

"St. Louis. Pit stop, you need anything or want to use the ladies' room?" Demetrius answered but didn't look at me.

"Um, no. I'm okay." I stretched a bit more. "Malachi?"

"He is inside paying for the gas." He sat stone straight and facing forward.

"Okay. I think I will get out and stretch a bit." I didn't know what Demetrius' problem was, and I would not pry.

"Go for it," he said and still didn't turn to watch as I got out of the car.

I stepped outside, and the frigid January air assaulted my body. The temperature had seriously plummeted, which was odd, considering we were heading south. I pulled my jacket closed and bounced around in hopes to generate some heat. As I bounced around in a circle, I noticed Malachi approaching me. His hood covered his head and threw a shadow across his face.

I smiled at him, but in return I received a frown and eye roll. I stopped bouncing and shot him a questioning glare, which he ignored and stepped past me to fill the tank. He set the nozzle in the opening, engaging the autofill, and walked a few feet away from the car. Tired of the cold shoulder that did nothing but add to the chill I already felt, I hopped back inside the vehicle.

"What is his problem?" I asked more to myself, but Demetrius answered it.

"He's upset," he responded simply.

"Yeah, that much is obvious." I looked back at the hooded figure outside of the car. "What's not obvious is why."

"You pulled from me instead of him." He turned, finally revealing his face to me.

The man looked downright exhausted. There were dark circles under his bloodshot eyes. His lips were dry from dehydration, and his shoulders slumped as if he'd been up for days.

"What?" Had I drained him of the life he had just hours before?

"While you were sleeping, you needed to rejuvenate, so you pulled from a male, and you pulled from me." He gave a weak smile that was both happy and apologetic.

"Wait, what are you talking about? I didn't touch you!" I denied everything, even though the evidence sat right in front of me.

"You don't have to touch me to siphon from me, Syrinada, and you pulled from me. You sang your serenade, a small moaning lullaby, and we thought he would be the one to respond, but I was. For the last few hours, you have been humming the lullaby and pulling energy from me. You pulled so much I didn't have the energy to drive anymore, so Malachi took over."

"Oh my god. I can't imagine what he must be going through right now! I didn't know. There is no way I would have done that if I had known." I shook my head. "He has to know that. Why is he so mad at me? I would never have done that to him on purpose."

"Syrinada, Malachi is not mad at you. He is just upset at the situation. It is a tough time for him." Demetrius turned and slumped back into his seat. "I'm sure you can understand why."

"Yes, I do." I peered again out the back window at Malachi, who had his back to us. "I can't imagine having him sit through that all this time. Fuck! Why is this so damn messed up?" I punched the back of the driver's seat, and Demetrius seemed to be amused by my show of frustration.

"I can't answer that." He turned around, dropped his head back against the headrest, closed his eyes, and yawned.

"This changes nothing between you and me, okay? Just because my body is, for whatever reason, drawn to you doesn't mean my mind is. It doesn't mean I will be with you." I made the declaration as if it were what he needed to hear, but really, I was the one who needed it. Truthfully, I wasn't sure if any of it was true. I couldn't trust myself, awake or not.

"I would expect no such thing from you." Demetrius sighed.

Malachi, who looked over his shoulder to catch my eye through the rear window, smiled, forever trying to protect me and spare my feelings. Yeah, and if I hadn't felt like shit before that, well grab the Pooper Scooper.

CHAPTER 15

Malachi returned to the car. He didn't speak to either of us; he just pulled his seat belt on, put the key in the ignition, and started the engine. We drove in an unnerving, awkward silence for hours until we reached the next pit stop, where Demetrius decided he would be the one to gas up the car and grab some snacks. He was starving, and his eyes widened when he saw the Burger King attached to the gas station. He took our orders and quickly hopped out of the car, rambling on about his craving for onion rings.

"Malachi," I said his name, testing if he would speak to me.

"Yes, Sy," he said through a tight jaw.

"I am so sorry, and I know you told me never to say that to you again, but I really am sorry. I can't even begin to—" Malachi held his hand up to stop my lengthy apology and spoke with his back to me, hood still covering his head.

"I don't want you to apologize to me. What I want is to take you away from all of this, from the danger and from Demetrius. I want to have you all to myself and forget that any of this ever happened. It killed me to have to sit here and watch as his body fed yours and to hear you call out for more in those soft moans. To feel the energy that passed between you was like murder, Sy!" He placed his hand on the steering wheel, gripping it tightly. "It broke me, and I couldn't understand why. If you aren't bonded to me, there is no way I should experience physical pain from another male giving to you. Yeah, I can understand being upset, annoyed, maybe even pissed off, but I felt like it was cutting through me. It's not right, but I think I get it now."

"Get what?" I whispered. He was completely open to me, vulnerable, and I couldn't interrupt that. I had to let him speak the words he needed to.

"You haven't bonded to me, but through some twisted turn of events, I have bonded to you. My body and soul belong to you, even though you remain free from me. Demetrius is older and stronger. Of course, you pulled from the strongest male near you. It's not how things typically work, but you are separate from us, free from the laws that bind our kind." He finally turned to look at me, and his eyes were dark and heavy with sadness.

"What does that mean?" I shuddered as he watched me.

What he said was true; I could feel it in his gaze. Malachi had paired with me. I remembered it from the books he gave me to read. It was hardly an insignificant occurrence, not like picking a boyfriend or girlfriend. It was deeper, and with sirens and mermen, it was an eternal promise. There he was, inside of this unbreakable bond, alone, because I didn't feel it on my end. Yes, I cared for him, but I could walk away if I wanted to. I still owned that choice. He no longer did.

"It means that I have to forget how things are supposed to be according to our history and accept how they are. You are different, and therefore, I must be as well." Once again, truth colored his words, and his eyes grew darker.

"I don't want him," I spoke of his brother, who had conveniently avoided being around for this conversation.

"You do, physically anyway, and perhaps more than that. Who knows, over time you may come to choose him over me." He gave a small hopeless chuckle.

He actually believed that I could choose his brother above him. Older and stronger. Yes, Demetrius had a lot of appeal, but I didn't know him, and I was already so close to Malachi. We'd been through so much together. It would take a lot more than a physical attraction for me to become attached to someone. It was possible that over time things could change the dynamic of our relationship, but I couldn't see that happening, or at least I didn't want to.

"I would never."

His jaw clenched tighter because he could hear the hesitancy in my tone, and I dropped my eyes from him. I was unsure, and that much was becoming more and more obvious.

"Don't make promises you can't keep, Sy." Malachi got out of the driver's seat, and his hood fell from his head, revealing a bald scalp.

"You cut your hair off?" I sat forward and gawked at his new appearance as he opened the back door. Don't get me wrong. Malachi still looked good without his hair, but I wasn't expecting it. Just hours ago, he was sporting long locs that hung halfway down his back.

"Yes." He examined my reaction and then gave me a small smile. Yeah, he realized I still found him attractive. Hell, the hair didn't make the alpha.

"When?" I asked and couldn't stop myself from biting my bottom lip.

"After I watched your hands reach out and touch his. At the last rest stop I snagged some clippers, and well, this is my new look, I guess." He rubbed his hand across his bare head and chuckled lowly.

"Oh, well, I wish it were under better circumstances, or for a better reason, but I like it. You look hot." I smiled at him, and my fingers gripped the seat. All I wanted to do was to allow my hands to follow the same path across his head.

"Thanks," he said simply and climbed into the back seat with me.

"What are you doing?" I moved back across the seat as he pulled my legs up to drape across the width of the SUV.

Malachi looked me in the eye as his fingers worked to unbutton my pants. He paused, waiting for my approval, and I nodded for him to continue. He slid the jeans down to my knees and moved his hand to free himself. The entire time he held my gaze with those intense and darkly saddened eyes. His arm slipped around my waist as he pulled me across the seat and turned me to my side so my ass was against his thighs.

My name slid across his lips like butter in a soft moan as he shifted his weight, rubbing his dick against me. I shifted, leaving my ass against him but twisting my waist so I could see him better. Seeing the desire in his eyes made my pussy quiver. Once in a suitable position, he slipped inside me. With each inch of his heat, I bit harder into my bottom lip.

Fully submerged inside of me, he leaned forward, pressing his lips to mine. "I want you," he whispered against my lips.

"You have me," I whispered back. "Take me."

His hips moved in response. With each slow thrust, he reached deeper inside of me. My breath stuttered. My chest warmed, and I struggled to remain in control of myself.

"Syrinada," Malachi spoke my name, still stroking. "You're safe with me. Now and forever. I will protect you. Do you understand that?"

"Yes," I moaned as the climax built.

"Good. Feed," he ordered, the authority of his alpha vibrating his voice.

The orgasm burst through my body in electric pulses. I gripped his arms, digging my nails into his flesh, and cried out. Malachi kept going. Pushing through my orgasm, he leaned into me as his pace quickened, and each thrust took more power. I grabbed his newly shaved head, pulling his lips back to mine. Something changed when our lips met.

I opened my mouth to call out his name, but instead of a call of ecstasy, I heard a song. It was nothing like the boisterous tone of my siren call, but softer, sweeter, a lullaby. Malachi continued to stroke me as I sang for him. I looked at him and smiled as I witnessed a single tear slide down his face. There was nothing left between us.

The situation was shitty as hell, but Malachi would remain by my side. This I knew. I promised him in that moment that I would never hurt him. With my eyes, I told him he was mine forever. With my touch, I told him that no other would be to me as he was, and as I hummed my lullaby, I told the world that Malachi was mine.

CHAPTER 16

*W**hen Demetrius returned to the car,** he found us sitting together in the back seat. He shot us a smile, but when he turned away, I could feel the tension fill his body. The smell of what we did still flooded the car. He gripped the steering wheel tightly as he opened all the windows, allowing the frigid wind to wash the air clean.

Malachi noticed his brother's anger as well, so he slid closer to me, as if he were claiming his territory. I rolled my eyes and ignored them both for a while. There was only so much I could handle, and I didn't enjoy being put in between two men, especially brothers. I popped a fry into my mouth and stared out the window as the car pulled off.

When we arrived in New Orleans, I had been asleep, and thankfully, no nonsense had occurred while I was out, and if it did, no one told me. I woke up wrapped in Malachi's arms. He kissed me on the top of my head and tightened his hold on me before he allowed me to move away.

"We're here." He smiled and pointed out the window to a large house.

"And where is here?" I yawned and stretched the knot out of my back.

"This is our home here in New Orleans," he said with pride. As I peered out at the large house, I understood why. The place was awe-inspiring. A large porch wrapped around the white house, holding up black and gray pillars that carried the second and third-floor balconies. The feeling that emanated from the house reminded me of a book I read and loved called *Mahogany Sin,* written by a local Chicago author who I had met just days before my world imploded.

Had I known my life was about to turn into material fit for a paranormal read, I would have asked her more questions. That reminded me, if I ever saw Latasha again, I would have to put her in a choke hold until she handed over my copy. Borrow my ass. That girl was a total book thief!

The second-floor balcony wrapped around the left side of the house and set out over the beautifully vibrant garden. Even in the setting sun, the flowers were still in full bloom. Guarded by an iron fence, the house sat on the street in nearly complete solitude. There weren't many structures remaining along the roads we followed to get there. Malachi would later explain that the storms had pummeled this area, but siren magic kept his house in near pristine condition.

"So, no cozy B&B?" I smiled as I stepped out of the car and stretched my limbs.

"Unfortunately, no. This house has been in our family for a very long time. Don't be surprised if it is covered in grime on the inside. I can't remember the last time anyone was actually here, and you will have to prepare any meals you desire all by your lonesome." He laughed.

"That's fine, as long as you have no plans of putting me on cleaning duty." I laughed and followed him inside.

"You, clean? Never!" He chuckled as he disappeared through the door and called back, "I wouldn't dare ask you to dirty your hands!"

The interior of the home took my breath away. Their house in Chicago was beautiful, but it paled compared to this one; even covered in its thin layer of gray film, it was magnificent. A grand staircase welcomed us in the large foyer, above a long hall that split off in seven different directions. Malachi disappeared up the stairs, but I didn't follow him. I couldn't help myself.

I roamed the halls and absorbed as many details of the home as I could. There were so many details that would absolutely end up on the pages of my sketch pad. From the carvings on the furniture, to the antique fixtures and paintings, it felt like I had stepped back in time. The momentary time travel was welcome because the present seriously sucked. I ran my hand along the furniture and let my mind wander.

I didn't know where Malachi had disappeared to, or where Demetrius was hiding, but neither query mattered much to me. It was better to be by myself and not have to worry about their issues on top of my own. Having them near me was much more of a headache than it felt like it was worth.

I enjoyed Malachi, the way I felt around him, how my body and mind responded to his presence. However, the moment his brother came into view, all that changed. Malachi's insecurities were a total turn off; it was no wonder why I had such a physical response to Demetrius. He was confident and secure; regardless of who else was around, Malachi lacked that.

Mentally, I wanted nothing to do with Demetrius. Yes, my stomach jumped a bit, and I felt that special response between my legs whenever he came near. But that was all physical, and it had become more than clear to me that my physical responses weren't exactly trustworthy. Either way, I would keep my distance from Demetrius. I would be sure to have encounters with him only when absolutely necessary.

I heard Malachi calling my name from somewhere on the opposite side of the house, and I purposely moved away from the sound of his voice instead of answering him, as I should have. He would find me eventually; the place wasn't *that* big. I wanted to prolong my moment of mental solidarity.

That last doorway at the end of the long hall opened to a small room. In the room was nothing but a candle covered alter and a narrow door. Compared to the rest of the house, the decor was a letdown. It didn't look like it belonged to the house, as if they installed it long after the beautiful pillars, tall ceilings and maze-like halls were constructed.

My nerves rattled as I approached the door. I'd spent what felt like hours searching the home and now a mystery stood in front of me. Curiosity was at an all-time high, and this door only fed into it. I wanted to open it, to peek in and see what they stored on the other side, but it disappointed me to realize that there was no knob.

My curiosity would have to go unsatisfied. Instead, I ran my hand along the thick wood, admiring the lining, but jumped back when I felt the pulse beneath my palm.

"What the hell?" I looked at my hand and then back to the knob-less door. As disturbing as it felt, something inside of me urged me to return my hand to the surface. So, I did.

First with my right hand, within seconds, the wood was pulsing against my palm again. The strange feeling turned comforting, and before I knew it, my left hand touched the surface. My hips swayed, shifting to the rhythm of the pulses. My eyes closed as the hypnotic pulse became music to my body. Each beat was a drum that fed the motion of my form.

I was in full trance when I heard Demetrius clear his throat behind me. I stopped and dropped my hands from the door but didn't turn to him. The heat of embarrassment flushed my cheeks, and I couldn't let him witness that.

"Why did you stop?" Demetrius asked.

"I thought I did something wrong." I got my voice in check. No trembles or signs of the internal freak out that was happening. "This doesn't exactly look like a location that is open to visitors."

"Ah, contrary to that, it is very much open to visitors, especially to you." He walked up behind me, and I stayed still as I felt the warmth of his body press against my back. He didn't touch me, but he was so close I could hear his soft breath and feel the air he expelled brush against my neck. "This is a place to become one with nature. Nothing is ever wrong with communing with Mother Earth."

"Is that what I was doing?" My breath was shallow, and as hard as I tried to conceal it from him, I knew he was aware of the effect he had on me.

"Yes. They carved the wood for this door from one of the oldest Oak trees ever to root here in New Orleans' soil. They say the tree took the magical properties of the land into it. The women of our family used to do the very thing you were just doing." He grabbed my hand and placed it back against the door. "They came here to connect with Mother Nature. Feel her energy, Syrinada. Let your own intertwine with hers and become one. Now is the time for you to let go, be free, and let your body react naturally. Close your eyes and enjoy it."

With my eyes shut as he suggested, I inhaled the deep scent of Oak and Earth and released it in a breathy tremble. In a moment, the pulsing started again. Only, it was much more intense. The vibrations radiated up my arms and through my body. It created a rhythmic humming in my mind that made me feel detached from my body.

When I could no longer feel the beating cadence beneath my skin, my eyes opened to find the world around me had vanished. In the dark space I was alone, but I felt oddly at peace. I walked around this place of nothingness, lit only by distance candlelight, and I felt amazing. I could still hear the rhythm of the Oak in my head and leaned into the sound. The volume increased, becoming a private concert that I swayed my hips and bobbed my head to.

"It's beautiful, isn't it?" His voice called from behind me, interrupting my moment. "Total solace, total peace."

A little irritated, I turned to face him. My jaw damn near hit the floor when I found a very naked Demetrius standing in front of me.

"What is going on?" I stepped back and looked around us, afraid I would see Malachi. If he found us, either it would kill him, or he would kill Demetrius. Neither option was ideal.

"You pulled me in here with you, Syrinada." Demetrius smiled and crept toward me.

"What?" I took another step in retreat from his approach.

Considering the rock hard body in front of me, and the instant arousal, it was difficult to move away from him. Already, I wasn't sure how much longer I could resist him. How was it

I couldn't feel my body before, but the moment I laid eyes on him, I became highly aware of the moisture between my thighs?

My eyes completed a happy and satisfied journey across his deep brown skin. I licked my lips absentmindedly as he moved, and his muscles flexed. Strong thighs, V-cut, eight-pack abs, broad chest, and pecks that looked capable of dancing beneath my palms. His locs fell around his face, down across his chest and shoulders, and I thought of Malachi's long hair he had chopped off because of my appreciation for his brother's. There was that pang of guilt I'd been missing.

Demetrius walked over to me and placed his hand on my cheek. "You called me to you, and I answered that call. Your siren is strong, and your will is my command to obey." He slowly slid his hand down my face to caress my neck, shoulder, and breasts, which I hadn't realized were bare. "You are so beautiful, Syrinada."

"This can't happen." Unsteady legs carried me away from him again, but he followed my motion effortlessly, not allowing for my retreat.

"It's happening because you want it to." He leaned in and slowly brushed my cheek with his lips.

"No, what about Malachi?" I turned my face from his kiss, and he groaned softly with disappointment.

"Ah, my brother." Demetrius fell to his knees in front of me. "Whatever will happen there?"

He didn't let me answer his question, nor did he allow for my protest of his actions. His hand gripped the back of my knee before he lifted my right leg and draped it over his shoulder. I watched in conflicted anticipation as he pressed his lips against the inside of my thigh. He left a trail of passionate kisses that covered my skin, getting closer to my pussy.

A soft hum passed his lips as he looked up at me. A pause that gave me one opportunity to stop him. I didn't.

The hungry grin stretched across his face before he disappeared between my legs. Demetrius stroked his tongue against my clit in such enthusiastic exploration that my body seized instantly. Within moments, I was calling out in ecstasy. All my resistance to him shattered completely as my spine arched and my body trembled with pleasure.

My hands clutched the sides of his head and pulled his face closer to me, urging him to continue. I didn't want the feeling to end. I was ready for more of him, ready to for his hands and lips to explore more of my body, and to have more than just his tongue between my legs.

However, that would never happen, because the place of nothingness that hid our forbidden moment of pleasure suddenly snapped back into being everything that was real and painful. I opened my eyes and turned from the door just in time to see Malachi's fist land square into his brother's jaw.

"What the fuck do you think you're doing?" Malachi yelled as Demetrius pulled himself up from the floor where he landed. "You're fucking low for this, D!"

"What's going on?" I asked Malachi. I didn't want them to be fighting, but I was also embarrassed because I understood from his expression that Malachi knew exactly what had just happened. He knew where my mind was, the thoughts I'd given into.

"I'm sorry, but it's pretty obvious who she chooses in reality," Demetrius growled and rubbed his jaw. His other hand hung in a tight fist at his side, as if he wanted to strike back but was resisting.

"Oh, okay, so because you know you can't have her in real life, you take it upon yourself to mind fuck her?" Malachi looked more than ready to take on his brother in a fight.

"What?" I grabbed his arm and pulled him back as I stepped forward to confront Demetrius. I didn't need Malachi to fight my battles for me, especially when someone was obviously taking advantage of me and in such a fucked-up manner. "What the fuck is he talking about?"

"Yes, Sy, my brother knew exactly what he was doing!" Malachi retorted from behind me when Demetrius neglected to respond to my question. I shot him a glare, and I felt him seize beneath it. I caught him in a lie, and there was nothing he could do to deny it. The truth of his brother's words tattooed the guilt in his expression.

"Wait, that was real? I thought I just imagined—" My face turned red. "That was real!"

"Yes, it was," Malachi confirmed.

"He said... he said it was my choice and that my body called him inside." I turned back to look at Malachi, afraid I would find hatred in his eyes, but what I saw there was much worse. Pity.

He felt bad for me. Why wouldn't he? On top of being used, my naivety of this new world left me vulnerable to being lied to and manipulated. Still, I didn't like being pitied. I was stronger than he gave me credit for, and I could already see that would be our biggest problem.

"That's total bull. They used that door and many like it for mates who had to be away from each other. It was mostly used during the time of the war with the covens," Malachi explained the history. "This way, if a siren were weak, she could still commune with her mate without having to take the risk of traveling through dangerous territories. It's called the Mate's Doorway."

"Are you serious?" I turned to Demetrius, who wore a strange combination of pride and shame in his expression.

"Yes, it's the truth, but what he is leaving out is that it wouldn't have worked if you didn't want me on some level." Demetrius puffed his chest, and Malachi growled.

"I don't give a fuck what you say Demetrius. This is some bull! Yeah, we all understand on some level she wants you, but not on a level that counts, or you wouldn't have had to pull this shit! How could you do this to me?" Malachi yelled at his brother, completely unable to hold back his anger and disappointment.

"To you? Are you fucking kidding me? I am trying to be patient and understanding, but damn!" Demetrius calmed himself before continuing. "Look, I know you are closer to her, and she knows you. Your time together resulted in a genuine connection with her. I get that, but I have been watching over her for years! A lot longer than you have. I have been taking care of this woman for so long, waiting for her to see me, but knowing that for her safety that could never happen. Now here she is, in my world, and she is tied to you, my brother!"

"Oh, boo fucking hoo! That's not an excuse for tricking her to mate with you!" Malachi yelled.

"Look, Syrinada, I apologize. What I did was low and dirty, but you have to understand how long I have wanted this, how many times I fantasized about it. Do you realize how insanely happy I was when Malachi called me with the news of you? I couldn't wait to get back, and then when I did, I find this." He pointed to his brother. "You and him mating, paring, and bonding. Him, not me!"

Demetrius's words were too intense and revealed a lot more than I was prepared for. I didn't know if the idea of him watching over me and lusting after me for so long should turn me on or off. On one hand, I felt bad that he was hurting, but on the other, I wasn't sure what that meant in terms of my life. My priority was not protecting the feelings of these men.

I looked at Malachi, who stared at his brother in understanding. They were both suffering the same torture; me. Knowing what he felt didn't really change anything. Yes, it made it easier to understand him, but it also made it harder to be around him. I thought about what Malachi said about me possibly getting to know Demetrius and falling for him. That was what Demetrius was waiting for.

"I need to get out of here," I spoke and moved past Demetrius and out of the small room.

"Where are you going?" he called after me.

"I don't know, but I can't be here with you right now!" I heard Malachi coming after me, so I turned to stop his debate, but he hadn't intended to argue with me. His hand hung between us, with keys dangling from his fingers.

"We stored this location in the GPS. Just select home, and it will bring you back to us." He dropped the keys into my hand. "If you need anything, there is money in the glove compartment. Use cash only so you can't be traced."

"Thanks," I said, confused that he would so easily let me leave. Then I saw it in his eyes, and the eyes of Demetrius behind him. They needed to be away from me just about as much as I needed to be away from them, maybe even more so. They needed to work this out between themselves like brothers and without the scent of my confused hormonal patterns clouding their judgment. I shot Malachi a small, apologetic smile before I left and headed for the front door of the house.

CHAPTER 17

I found out just how beautiful New Orleans could be when given the chance to explore it. I could understand why so many people talked about getting lost in the magic of it all. Yes, there were a lot of homes that had never recovered from hurricane Katrina. Driving through the streets, I found there was so much that brought the FEMA commercials to mind. My heart went out to everyone who had lost friends, families, and homes in the disaster.

The land itself, however, was recovering, and the spirit of the people was still very much alive. As the sun slipped from the sky, the streets erupted with lights, music, and delicious smells that made my mouth water. I stopped at a small restaurant called Court of The Two Sisters. The smell of catfish and gumbo called to me. I walked up to the door and peeked inside but saw that every table was full, and the host was telling a tall, slender man in a blue suit that the wait would be at least two hours. I turned to leave, hoping to find somewhere more accessible because I didn't have that type of patience.

"Why are you leaving so soon?" a soulful voice with that classic southern-bell twang sounded off behind me like the song of a bird.

"I'm not up to a two-hour wait." I turned to the woman, who was simply radiant.

She was at least a foot taller than me, and her skin was a silky tan that was barely covered by the green, strapless, knee-length dress she wore. She had enormous eyes surrounded by thick, curly lashes and pouty lips. Yeah, she was gorgeous, and the way she batted her long lashes was nearly hypnotic, even for me. She brushed back a strand of her auburn hair behind her ear; the rest of her mane was pulled up into a tight bun atop her head.

"Oh, that wait time is not for *you*." She looped her arm through mine and pulled me back into the restaurant. "Table for *two*," she said, and the staff seemed dazed. The server took the menus she had just given to a young couple and gave them to us. "I'm Verena, glad to meet you." She smiled at me.

"Syrinada," I responded as we sat down. "How did you do that?" I watched the team rush to fill our water glasses and replace a flower that didn't need to be replaced. Anything to make her happy, it seemed.

"Syrinada, ooh, I love that name! Let me guess, you're a newbie to the siren game." She spit out the fact about me as if it were common knowledge and continued talking, ignoring the wide eyes of disbelief on my face. "Isn't it funny how many of our mamas tried to hide it from us. I mean, obviously we would all come to figure it out." She lifted an empty glass, which the server filled with wine before she even had to ask.

"Yeah, obviously." I chuckled and played along. Because as beautiful as she was, that was already wearing off. I didn't trust her. Verena gave me a bad feeling. I couldn't be too open with anyone, especially another siren.

Even though we hadn't placed an order, they covered the table with treats. I was sure the food belonged to other patrons who, if we were in Chicago, would have been shooting us dirty looks. Instead, they went on with their conversations as if nothing were out of sorts.

I ate because my stomach growled, and the food smelled too good to pass up. I listened as Verena told me how she found out about her siren side and all the new tricks and tips she could share with me. Verena enjoyed playing with men, pissing off women, and getting what she wanted. By the time the meal ended, I was stuffed and tired of listening to her rambling.

Her attitude about it all sickened me as I compared her to the women who started the wars with the witch covens. Verena hopped up and headed away from the table before the check even came, and when it didn't arrive, I took out some cash and left it on the table. I wasn't sure how much all the food cost since we hadn't exactly looked at the menus the hostess gave us, but I was not about to dine and dash.

Verena waited for me outside of the restaurant, but as I came to the door, a tall man called her name, and she skipped across the street to answer him. I hurried and jumped into the car and drove away before she could come back. I had no desire to continue talking to her or accompany her to the many clubs she rambled on about frequenting. Lucky for me, her distraction freed me of having to come up with an excuse for why I just had to be anywhere else, anywhere else, but with her.

Three hours later, I came to the end of an abandoned street. With no other cars around, I just sat and stared at the steering wheel. It was time for me to go back to the house. My mind was buzzing with the images, sights, sounds, and tastes of New

Orleans. The feeling was euphoric, and I didn't want it to end, but going back there would erase any of the thrill I felt.

But I had to go back. After the meal with Verena and the shopping I couldn't help doing afterward, there was only a few dollars left in the glove compartment, and my wallet was back at the house in my bag that I forgot to grab when I made my hasty escape. Without the sun, the area looked a lot scarier. The last thing I wanted to do was run out of gas and have to walk back to the house. I tapped the screen of the GPS and started the navigation back to the brothers.

As I maneuvered the car to make a U-turn, the headlights swept across a man who turned to look at me. I recognized him immediately. The last time I saw him he was a gangly mess, wearing dirty clothes, covered in sweat, and most likely a few other unnamed bodily fluids. He was high as hell and climbing out of a car with his other slum bag friends.

I couldn't believe it. I slammed on the brakes and watched him. My blood boiled. I'd left Chicago to get away from what they'd done to me, and that asshole had the nerve to be in New Orleans! It wasn't a coincidence; he followed me. Why else would he be there? Since he wanted me so badly, I'd make his wish come true. I whipped out my cell phone and called Malachi.

"Hello?" Malachi picked up after the second ring.

"I'm about to do something bad." I hung up, cutting off his string of follow-up questions that had already begun. There was no time for questions, and I wasn't hiding. He could find me; he always had.

I let the car enter a slow roll and followed the man until he figured out that his dumb ass was being tailed and ran. As he attempted to dash across the street to the narrow alley, I spun the car in front of him, and he ran headfirst into the tail. I got out of the driver's seat and walked around to where he was lying on the ground. He looked up at me, nose and right eye bleeding from the impact.

"How did you find me, man? She said I would be safe down here." He groaned as he attempted to stand and fell, holding his ankle, which had twisted when he hit the car.

"Apparently not safe enough!" I stomped on the ankle he was babying, and he cried out.

"Look, I'm sorry. Don't fuck me up like you did my boys. The woman had cash, man, a lot of it; she said we just had to mess with you a bit, nothing major. We didn't touch you like that. I swear!" he cried his confession.

I wanted to kill him. What the fuck did he mean they didn't touch me like that? As if I didn't remember his ring leader's hands on me, the stench of his breath, the gross feeling of his blood on my face. Instead of killing him right then for his stupid statement, I stomped down on the raw ankle that was already swelling and smiled as he screamed from the pain.

"What woman?" I growled, and I could feel the surrounding atmosphere change as the wind suddenly kicked up. This was my father's bloodline, pure magic. I took a deep breath and tried to remain calm. I had no idea what I was doing or how to control it.

"Look, I am so sorry. I saw what you did to them. I just... I don't want to end up that way." Tears streamed down his face, mixing with the snot from his nose. "Fuck, she promised me I would be safe down here!" He begged before screaming out as the heel of my boot dug into his flesh.

"Who the fuck is *she?*" I twisted my foot, adding more pressure to his ankle until the bone snapped and gave way beneath my weight. He cried out and rolled around the ground. "Talk! You better tell me right now! Or I can start in on the other one."

"The woman from the retirement home! I don't know why she stays over there with all those old heads, but whatever, she had cash money and a picture of you. She said she didn't want us to seriously hurt you, but that it was time. She kept saying it was time but wouldn't tell us time for what."

I stepped back from him and ran my hands through my hair. It couldn't be. He had to be lying to me, spewing out a false cover story someone else told him to say if he ever got caught and questioned. I kicked him in the side and yelled, "You better not be lying to me!" I kicked him again, and he coughed up blood. "Is it true?"

"Yes! I swear! Please don't hurt me! She gave us the photo, address, and exact time you would be there. It was all a setup!" He held out his hands, pleading for me to end my assault.

"Sy! Stop!" Malachi called as he jumped out of a small black car that hadn't yet come to a complete stop. Once the car was parked, Demetrius hopped out, hot with rage.

The older brother ran in front of me and approached the junkie whose name I hadn't gotten. Demetrius was ready to defend me if necessary. I watched him, a true predator, strong and concentrated on his target, and I almost voiced my appreciation for him. Almost. Instead, I looked away from him to Malachi.

"What happened here?" Malachi asked, rolling his eyes at his brother's display.

"This is one of them, the asshole who snatched me up!" I couldn't disguise the venom in my tone. If they hadn't shown up when they did, this nameless junky would have met an ending like his friends.

"Seriously?" He peered at the bloody man. "Are you sure?"

"Yes, and if what he is saying is true, I know who set me up." My jaw tightened because there wasn't enough of me that doubted what the man had confessed to me. "I know who did this to me!"

"What do you mean?" Malachi took a step toward the man who looked terrified of Demetrius, who was still focused on the broken man. "Did this asshole say something to you?"

"Yeah, says someone paid them off to snatch me up and scare me, but not to hurt me. Whatever the fuck that means, considering what they did! He said it was a woman who lives in a senior community who gave them cash to do her bidding. A woman who clearly doesn't belong in a senior community." I looked Malachi directly in the eye. "Sound like anyone you know?"

"Shit, Noreen did this to you?" Demetrius stood from his crouched position. The man was no real threat to anyone.

"It appears so," I answered through gritted teeth, as I felt the familiar tingle of the magic in my blood stirring. Demetrius and Malachi kept a watchful eye on me as I tried to calm the rising anger.

"Look, we have to go. Throw his ass in the car, and we can question him back at the house," Demetrius spoke up.

"Yeah, we need to be sure what he is saying is the truth. We can't jump to any conclusions on this." Malachi rubbed my arm with his hand and tried to console me, but we both knew what the truth was.

The description the crackhead gave was too spot-on for it to be anyone but my aunt. Now I understood the twisted feeling in my gut the last time I was with her. Family or not, it was everything in me telling me the bitch was not to be trusted!

Demetrius tossed the nameless man in the car's trunk. The guy didn't even fight; It probably relieved him to be away from me. Demetrius barely looked at either his brother or me as he told us he would meet us back at the house. I hopped in the passenger seat, because neither of us trusted my ability to drive. Once inside the vehicle, we didn't move. We sat there, parked awkwardly across the deserted block.

"What happened between you two after I left?" I asked him before he could bring the conversation back to my backstabbing aunt.

"We talked," he answered simply.

"I assumed that much." I leaned back in the seat and waited for him to give a more detailed response.

"Yeah. Look, this obviously isn't easy on any of us. To avoid unnecessary tension, we agree that for now, the focus will remain on protecting you, not to mate with you, or to stake a claim. That goes for both of us." Malachi peeked at me from the corner of his eye.

"And that means what, exactly?"

"It means we won't interact with you on a physical level or any other way outside of the professional necessity to protect you either in reality or through subconscious passages," he stated it as a fact as if it was being read off a piece of paper. Law.

"Oh." I wasn't sure how I felt about that.

There was that selfish part of me that was upset because this little deal of theirs also meant they cut me off. The logical part of my brain understood it was the right thing to do. It was the best decision, considering that the idea of settling down with either of them wasn't one that excited me. Bonded for life. Hell, that was too much to contemplate with everything else that was happening. They knew how fucked up my life was. Why would anyone want to be bonded to it?

"I met another siren tonight." I opted to change the topic than to voice my concerns.

"Yeah?" He turned on the engine and shifted the gear into drive. I thought he would have more concern about another siren, but he showed little interest.

"Verena. An odd girl." I thought about the woman who I left standing on the street talking to a man in the shadows.

"Oh, well, maybe you should lie low for a while. We don't exactly want the covens getting tipped off about your location."

"I hadn't thought of that." I frowned and looked out the window as he started the engine. It wasn't as if I trusted Verena, but I hadn't considered that she could have ties to the covens. After hearing about my aunt, anything was possible. If my own family could betray me, anyone could.

"Yeah, neither did I. Clouded judgment," he mumbled as the car pulled forward.

"Right." Well, at least that wouldn't be a problem anymore. Sure, practicing abstinence with a hormone driven siren wasn't a total recipe for disaster!

CHAPTER 18

ack at the house, Malachi and Demetrius thought
it best to keep me separated from my former attacker.
Demetrius, unlike me, thought to ask his name. Mark. The man
who took part in ruining my life's name was *Mark*! I don't know
why, but his generic name pissed me off even more.

When we entered the front doors, Malachi ushered me in
one direction, while Demetrius dragged Mark in another. He
rambled on about how he thought I would like the room they
picked out for me. It had the best view of the garden, and the
smell of the blossoming flowers filled the air.

"I thought we were going to be questioning his ass. Why am
I in here, Malachi?" I wanted one-on-one time with Mark.

"We are going to question him. You need to calm down first. There is no point in going out there all hot headed. You won't be able to focus on the information that matters. Odds are you will snap and end up killing him." He shook his head. "Hell, you already did a number on the guy."

"Well, can you blame me?" There it was again, that judgmental tone. At least I called him before I did anything. Didn't I at least get credit for that?

"No, I guess not, but action before thought doesn't exactly help us out in this scenario, does it?" Malachi doubled down with his all-knowing annoyance.

"Yeah, okay. I know you're right." Frustrated, I sat on the bed and dropped my head into my hands.

"Okay, so, we're going to stash him away and you're going to rest tonight. Together, and with clear heads, we'll question him in the morning." He double-checked the door, making sure it was secure, as if I didn't know how to operate a damn lock!

"No problem. I'm sure I will get a great night's sleep knowing that bastard is here."

"I figured you would have trouble, which is why I am going to stay here with you. To help you relax and to make sure you don't go looking for him in the middle of the night." He smiled;

proud that he had already considered all the angles. I saw little that he could do to help me relax after the new *no touch* policy.

"And how do you intend on helping me relax?" I challenged him. "I mean, I just found out that my own aunt, the woman who raised me as her daughter, set me up to have a bunch of fucked up men snatch me off the street and do God-only-knows what to me. Then she stood in my face and pretended not to know.

Here I was keeping my trauma to myself, not telling her because I didn't want her to worry about me and the entire time it was her doing! How could someone so close to me do something like that?" I moved from the bed and paced the floor because my frustrations, both physical and mental, were in a constant growth pattern. I couldn't be still; to be still was to be accepting of the bullshit.

"I honestly don't know what to say to you right now, because I know there is nothing I can say to make this better. What Noreen did was a complete and total betrayal of your trust, and that's putting it mildly." He watched me pace, and I could see his own struggle as he stood across the room from me.

The weight of his desire inspired images in my own mind. Flashes of kisses that covered my body, and his hands gripping my waist; my imagination went wild. I bit my lip because I knew none of it would be happening. He wouldn't allow it. I shook the thoughts and mental pictures from my mind.

"I just don't understand what my life is anymore. I am a half-siren, half-warlock mutt. My mother is dead, and my father is nowhere to be found. I feel completely out of control. Malachi, I hurt people, and I enjoy it. It is so weird to say this, but I think I looked forward to it." I returned to the bed.

"What did you look forward to?"

"When I saw him on the street, I was angry, yes, but there was also a part of me that was excited. It was like I'd just found my next target and wanted nothing more than to be the one to remove him from this world. That isn't me; at least it didn't use to be me. I don't know who I am anymore.

And now, the one solid part of my life, the part I thought would be there for me to fall back on and catch me when all this goes to hell, just crumbled in front of me! My own aunt, my family, set me up to be broken. I don't know what I did to her or what made her think I deserved any of this." Tears fell from my eyes, and as much as I hated the idea of crying in front of him, the release felt good. As the tears flowed, the tension in my chest eased, but a flood of sadness replaced it.

"You aren't deserving of this. No one is. Sy, you did nothing wrong. Whatever happened, whatever her reasons were for doing this, it says more about her and who she is as a person, than it does you. It doesn't define you, none of this does. What defines you, are your own actions. I know you have done some less than favorable things lately, but that is only because of the transition. You will find yourself again. Even if it is confusing now, you will remember who you are and what kind of person you are." Against the new policy, he crossed the room, pulled me from the bed and into his arms.

I laid my head on his shoulder. A hug didn't really break the rules, and I needed it. I needed more, but a hug was a good start.

"You cannot let this break you down," he continued. "As tempting as it may be to give up or give in to the urge to do the wrong thing, fight it."

"That is all so much easier to put into words than into action right now. All I want to do is find wherever you stashed that guy and... hell, I don't know what. I just know I don't want to have to sit here idly waiting to find out what I already know to be true." I pulled away from him and wiped my face on the back of my sleeve.

"We need to find out why she did what she did. I doubt she gave him much information as to the motivation behind her actions, but maybe she slipped up and said something, gave a clue that can help us. Either way, we have to be sure."

"Okay, you're right." I moved to sit in the old claw footed chair with the high back that was next to the large paned windows. "I'm not sure if I actually want to know why she did it or what her plan is now."

Outside the window, the wind howled, and I closed my eyes. I imagined I could attach myself to the current of the wind and let it carry me far away from my life. It would take me across oceans, deserts, and islands. It didn't matter the location if I could be free.

"We should have caught this. We didn't just watch you, we monitored her as well. The more I think about it, the more I'm sure I know where the problem stems from." He walked over to stand in front of me and leaned against the window, and with a somber tone he said, "I think I know who it is."

"You do?" I sat up in the chair. "Who?"

"If my suspicions are correct, Maurice. He's been head of security for a while now. If anyone should have picked up on any oddities in Noreen's patterns, it should have been him. He was the one who signed off on all reports before they came to me. He was the one who assigned the posts, and he was the one who was supposedly watching over you the night they snatched you." The muscles in his jaw tensed as he spoke, as if he couldn't stomach the betrayal. I knew exactly how he felt.

"You think he is in on this with her?" My brain worked to piece the puzzle together. It would make sense. Maurice clearly had an issue with me. I thought it was because of Malachi's affection for me, but perhaps it was something more.

"Unfortunately, I think so, and as many ways as I have tried to dispute it, it makes sense. Think about it, he was there at the house the night you escaped. I couldn't figure out how it took him so long to catch that." Malachi shook his head. "As if he really believed you were in the shower for that long! That shit made no sense, and now to find out about Noreen. He was closer to her than he should have been, and I had warned him about it before. Maybe their relationship was more than I had assumed." He glanced out of the window as if calculating the mistakes he had made.

"Relationship? You mean to tell me he and my aunt were together, as in physically?" I frowned, disgusted that they were together.

How could Noreen be with someone like Maurice? The man stunk of Beta. I remembered it all too well. It made my stomach turn. There was no way I would ever get close enough to give that odor a chance to cling to me.

"Yes, Noreen is a very alluring woman; one newbie caught him in the act with her and reported it back to Demetrius because he was too afraid to confront Maurice head on. We warned him it was against protocol and further indiscretion would result in him having to step down. He swore it was a onetime occurrence and that he would keep his distance. Since then, we thought we had settled the matter, as there were no further reports of him acting out of good conscience. Clearly, he found a way around our rules."

"Well, he was the head of surveillance. I'm sure it wouldn't have been that hard to work around a program he controlled. Even if you had others watching him, Noreen is a siren. Maybe she helped blind them to his actions." I sat back in the chair and sighed as my previous sadness and longing for a free-flowing existence once again solidified into a ball that rested in my chest.

"In hindsight, we should have taken him off the detail, but it was a first offense, and we had no reason not to trust him. It's not like it would be the first time a siren swayed a beta male, especially one like Maurice. He has always tried to prove himself worthy of a higher status. To have someone like Noreen show appeal for him, well, it would be hard to resist. Noreen is no beta siren. Not by a long shot."

"So, I think it's pretty damn obvious now that Maurice is banging my aunt and helped her set me up. What more do we need to know?" I ignored his high remarks about my aunt. Nice, she was a strong siren and high in the physical ranks for mating material.

So, the fuck what?

"We still need to know why they did it, and why Noreen, who is clearly at the top of the food chain, would lower herself to be with Maurice." Malachi softened. "It had to be something she seriously wanted in order for her to do that."

"That's true enough. Maurice isn't exactly appealing." I made a gagging noise and couldn't help the small laugh that followed it.

Malachi laughed. "Is that right?"

"Okay, it was harsh, but his scent is just weird. It's not even like the other males you know. They smell okay, but it's nothing like your alpha scent. It's like you make me horny, but they are only appealing if I'm already revved up and need a release. With Maurice, his scent is just wrong; it's more disturbing. The way he smells, it's putrid, like something pulled out of the bowels of a dead animal. I literally had to swallow back puke. I'm surprised any of you can stand it."

"Are you sure?" He stood up straight and stepped away from the wall he had been leaning on. "I mean, is that really your response to him or are you exaggerating?"

"Yes, why?" I stood up because his sudden movement and change in disposition jarred something inside of me. "Don't tell me this means something else is wrong we me. I just figured it was normal because he obviously didn't like me. Like it was one of those heightened senses. My siren abilities allowing me to smell his hatred for me. Am I not supposed to react that way to him?"

"You're supposed to be turned off, but not brought to a point of being physically ill." There was that tightness in his jaw line again.

"So, this means something more than just poor hygiene, I am assuming?" I swayed in a small tight pattern. I wanted to walk, to move, but there was nowhere to go.

"Yes, it does. It means we need to move faster. We don't have time to wait to see the seer. Demetrius is going to have to pull some strings. I need to go talk to him." He headed for the door.

"Why?" I stopped him with my question and chewed on my bottom lip, experiencing both fear and anxiety over what his answer might be.

"That scent, the one you described, if I am right, it means that he has been doing a lot more than getting down with your aunt," he growled, which caused me to flinch at the unexpected sound.

"You're going to have to give me a little more to go off than that."

"It just means that we need to figure out what the hell else he has been up to." Malachi grabbed the handle of the door. "I know I said I would stay with you, but please promise me you won't leave this room. I need to go talk to my brother," he said before he unlocked it.

"Okay, I promise." As much as I wanted to leave and be free, I didn't know what I would find out there if or when I did.

"I am serious, Sy. You can't leave this room," he repeated with his back to me.

"And I said I promise." I couldn't blame him; it wasn't like it would be the first time I had gone against his wishes.

"I'll come back when I'm done. It shouldn't take long," he said as he ducked out of the room.

I returned to the seat by the window and waited for him to return. Of course, my mind went on a race of unanswered questions and mounting concerns. There was more to the picture than I could see, and I felt like I was being smothered by all the unknown details. I tried not to contemplate what Malachi could have been thinking about Maurice and his concealed actions or motives. However, that was all I could think about. My aunt was banging a beta and planning my demise, but why?

CHAPTER 19

The night was long, and Malachi did not return as he promised he would. I sat by the window until the howling wind no longer brought me thoughts of a free-flowing spirit, but left me feeling like a caged animal. I showered and changed into clothes that were more comfortable and tried to read a book I had brought with me. It was a paranormal series about a girl who found out she was next in line to be queen of an alien race of vampires.

I was eager to continue reading it but was crushed when I realized I had grabbed the book three instead of book two from my shelf. I kicked myself and made a vow for the hundredth time that I would invest in a Kindle. Then I wondered if my new life would ever afford me the luxury of having real time to enjoy a book again. That simple pleasure that I had taken for granted. The way things were going, there was no way I could spend hours, or days, with my face buried between the pages of a book.

I wanted to go find Malachi to figure out what had happened, but I made a promise that I wouldn't leave the room, no matter what. For once, I wanted to keep my word. So instead, I busied myself with random workouts, self- care routines, and any other thing I could do while keeping my brain in an idle state. I didn't want to think too much, which wasn't easy, considering that I was a woman, a siren, and apparently in heat.

When I finally felt tired enough to sleep, I climbed into the bed beneath the plush white comforter. As I drifted off to sleep, I could hear a soft humming surround me. Briefly, I considered investigating the sound. I thought of pulling myself from the bed and searching the room for hidden speakers or passageways. But my body refused to give in to my mind, and a few moments later, I drifted to sleep.

"Sy!" Malachi was damn near sitting on top of me and shaking my body when my eyes opened. His figure was a frantic haze that confused the hell out of me. "Are you okay?"

"What? What are you doing?" I slapped his hands off my shoulders.

"You wouldn't wake up." He got off me and helped me sit up in the bed.

"Yeah, they definitely know we are here, we have to move." Demetrius stood from behind the bed, holding what looked like a black snake covered in orange slime.

"What the hell is that?" I jumped off the bed, getting as far away from the creepy thing as possible.

"This is a Sleeper. The witches used them to lull sirens so they were more vulnerable, using their own magic against them." He looked at Malachi. "You were right; we have to get her out of here. Get the car loaded. I'll make a few calls."

"Wait, what about Mark? I thought we were going to question him!" I turned on Malachi.

"Sy, there isn't time for all that. This proves everything we suspected is true. We need to go."

"And what, he just walks?" I pointed to the open door as if Mark stood there. "How do you know he won't go running back to my aunt and tell her everything?"

"Sy," Malachi spoke, but Demetrius interrupted him.

"No, she's right, which is why I am going to arrange for him to remain detained here in New Orleans, out of contact with your aunt."

"And who are you going to get to do that?" I rolled my eyes. "We already know we can't trust everyone on your team."

"Some are more deserving of trust than others," Demetrius defended.

"Okay, how do you know these people are deserving?" I bristled. "You were so sure Maurice was trustworthy, and the entire time he was sleeping with the enemy."

"They're family," Demetrius answered.

"Family." I returned my gaze to Malachi. "I thought you said you two were the last of your bloodline, no more family left."

"They aren't blood relatives, but they are family." Demetrius placed the sleeper in a small silver pouch and sealed it shut. "We grew up with them; they raised us after our parents died."

"Oh." My cheeks reddened with embarrassment.

"Look, we really need to get the hell out of here. If you have any other questions, we can answer them on the way." Demetrius walked out of the room.

"He is right." Malachi nodded before grabbing the bags I hadn't opened. "We have to get out of here. I'm not even sure how they got that damned thing in here. We checked everything when we arrived!"

"Looks like another inside job," I commented, and Malachi scoffed. "I'm not being a dick. We were all away from the house when you guys came and saved Mark's life. Maybe they did it then."

"Yeah. I think you might be right." He stared at me and then asked, "Are you okay?"

"Yeah, I mean, I was just sleeping, right?" I looked at the bed. "That thing, did it do anything to me? I don't feel any different."

"No, it didn't do anything. It just puts you in a deep sleep, gives a witch the time to get to you." He lifted the bags in his hands. "Do you need anything out of these bags to get ready to leave?"

"Um, no I guess not." I still had an open bag in the bathroom with my essentials.

"Okay, I am going to reload the car. You get ready, and I will come get the rest of your things for you."

"Yeah, okay." I plopped down on the bed as he picked up the bags and quickly carried them out of the room.

Once he was gone, I nervously checked around the room for any more Sleepers. Showering was fun. Instead of enjoying the soothing effect of the water, I was too busy scanning the area to make sure nothing was trying to sneak up on me. I spent so much time on patrol that I almost stepped out of the shower without rinsing the soap from my body. I quickly dressed and grabbed my bag because I was too nervous to wait for him to return, and I didn't want to leave it unattended. Yeah, paranoia had a tight grip around my ass.

I made it to the front of the house just in time to see Mark being loaded into the SUV, bound by ropes. He looked horrible enough, but when he saw me, his face when white with fear. I stopped and watched him closely as Demetrius pushed him back into the seat and the door closed.

Demetrius turned and looked at me. For a moment it looked like he would run away. The man didn't want to be around me alone. I was going to speak, try to break the tension, but he hurried and jumped into the driver's seat and started the engine. I froze because I wasn't sure if I should get in or not. It didn't seem to be a good idea to be locked away with either him or the hobbled man in the back.

I jumped as a hand squeezed my shoulder and turned to find Malachi, who stepped aside just in time to miss getting hit by the bag I had swung at him.

"Whoa! Calm down!" He held his hand up. "I come in peace."

"Shit! Don't do that, Malachi!" I readjusted the bag on my shoulder.

"Nervous?"

"You think?" As if waking up from a magic induce coma wasn't enough to put anyone on edge.

"It's okay." He looked me in the eye, searching for something. "We're leaving now. You're safe."

"Are we all riding in there together?" I pointed at Demetrius and his new pal, ignoring his claims of my safety.

"No, I doubt that will be a good idea." He pointed to the small car parked behind the SUV. "We'll take that one."

"Good." I peered into the backseat at Mark and bristled. Put me in the car with that man, and it would be murder.

When we got to the new house, I was speechless. This time not because of a grand appearance, but because of the dilapidated mess that sat in front of me. This house looked like it had taken all that the hurricane had to throw at it and barely survived. I sat in the car as they instructed me while they got Mark into his new hiding place and warned the family of my presence. Apparently, they were a feisty group who did not appreciate unannounced visitors.

On the way there, I asked more questions about the Sleepers and any theories about my enemy that Malachi had. He told me he was still positive that Maurice was in on it. He figured the traitor sounded the alarm the moment we left Chicago. They waited until we had all left the house to plant the Sleepers because they knew the brothers would have scrutinized every inch of the house when we first arrived.

A quick search after leaving my room, and they found those damn things under every bed and a few other hidden treats I surely would have passed out if I had seen. If Malachi had gone to bed before returning to my room, there was no way we would have gotten out of there before the witches caught up to us.

When Malachi left the car, he told me it would only be a few minutes. The clock revealed his lie. After twenty minutes, I was getting antsy, paranoid, and frustrated. Where were they? Had the witches found us? Were they somewhere fighting for their lives? Why wasn't I in there helping them?

I couldn't take it anymore. I got out of the car, and like a discount ninja, crept up to the house. The shabby structure sat behind a rusted fence with weeds growing out all around it. While I sat in the car, I imagined too many times that the damn things had grown since we got there and were reaching out for me. I had just laid my hand on the fence where they disappeared along the side of the house when a small voice stopped me in my tracks.

"Who are you, and what are you doing at my house?" I turned around to see a small woman who was nearly short enough to take the classification of dwarf. She was small but stocky, and her voice contradicted her strong frame and mean glare. She had long messy hair that covered her face and gave her an eerie look, almost as if she had just climbed out of a swamp, but had somehow shaken off all traces of mud.

"I, um, I..." I stuttered.

"Yeah? Spit it out already!" she demanded.

"She's with us, Aunt Tylia!" Demetrius appeared from behind the house, and as soon as she saw him, this burly little woman softened.

If I hadn't seen it with my own eyes, I would never have believed it. Her stocky frame thinned, and her movements were more fluid. Her face wore a soft smile and kind eyes. I could do nothing but gawk at her. Even her hair changed from the thick matted mess and sat in soft curls that framed her face and gave her an angelic look.

"Demi! My baby, you're here!" The little woman ran past me and jumped at Demetrius, who caught her midair and hugged her tightly. She played with his hair and nuzzled into his neck. Again, I just stared and gawked at the pair.

"Yes, I am." His face warmed with her hug. "I came to ask a favor."

"Yes, anything for you. Oh, where is your brother? Please tell me he is with you. It's been so long since I saw the two of you. My babies!" she squealed as he lowered her to the ground and stepped to the side so she could see Malachi, who was approaching behind him.

He smiled at me as the little woman shot off over to Malachi and repeated the same greeting. With Malachi, when she reached up to play with his locs, she frowned and smacked his head.

"Your hair! What happened to your hair?" She still nuzzled him but continued to smack his skull.

"Thought it was time for a new look." Malachi winced after she hit him again.

"Oh, *new*, that word." She frowned. "I hate that word! Everyone is always so concerned with things being new. Appreciate the old, I say!"

"Yes, I know, Aunt Tylia." He smiled at me around the old woman.

I just stared, completely awed by the display. Both brothers were so different around this woman. Neither had the edge I'd grown accustomed to. It was like they were free to be vulnerable around her.

"Who is she?" Tylia asked as she climbed down from Malachi.

"She is Syrinada, a siren, and she needs our help and yours right now," Demetrius spoke as Tylia approached me in her more favorable appearance.

I stood as still as the trees behind me. I was not sure why, but it felt like the best thing to do while she made her assessment of me. Behind her, the brothers looked as nervous as I felt. That couldn't be a good thing. She circled me and mumbled to herself as she looked me up and down.

I didn't know what she was thinking, but the whole thing was making me uncomfortable. I wanted to move away from her, but I didn't. There was something primal at work here. She was powerful, someone who commanded respect. I wouldn't step into her home and disrespect her, even if I didn't understand the customs.

"Syrinada," she said my name slowly and stopped in front of me. "I suppose."

That was it. She walked away and into the house. I thought it was a huge slap in the face, but the two of them were grinning like I had just received the greatest compliment possible from this little woman.

"What was that about?" I whispered the question, even though I was sure she was out of earshot.

"That was Tylia approving of you," Demetrius said with a small smile.

"Seriously? Hell, I thought she was going to attack me or something." I shook out my limbs from the frozen state they were in. "I wanted to move away, but I couldn't. At first it felt like it was my choice, but then, it was like I was being forced to stand there."

"Yeah, Tylia has her ways." Demetrius chuckled and followed the woman into the house.

"You okay?" Malachi asked as he approached.

"Yeah, I'm fine." I looked at the open door. "So, are we going in?"

"Yeah, when you're ready." He nodded.

"No time like the present, right?" I looked up at him.

Malachi grabbed my hand, threading his fingers with mine, and smiled. "You're going to do great."

Entering the house felt like crossing a barrier between realms. What looked like a broken-down shack on the outside was a beautiful home on the inside. It wasn't grand or overly done, but it was homey and comfortable. I didn't dare part my lips to ask what magic was used to create such an illusion. I just followed Malachi through the living room, which held plush furniture and a vast assortment of candles and trinkets.

We crossed the threshold into a small dining room where Demetrius sat stuffing his face, and Tylia pointed to two chairs for us. Seconds after we sat down, she was piling our plates with some of the best food I had ever tasted. She looked at me expectantly, and when the first spoonful passed my lips, I couldn't stop myself. I dove in. Satisfied by my reaction, Tylia took a seat and sat back to watch us eat. She didn't take one bite; it was as if the act of watching others as they enjoyed their meals was all that she needed to fulfill her.

When we finished our plates, Malachi smacked his stomach, pleased with the meal. Demetrius grinned and stretched his arms above his head. Tylia smiled and clapped her hands.

"Good, then." She stood. "Well, there is much to do. Demetrius, the boys will be here soon. Meet them outside, please."

"Yes." Demetrius nodded.

"Malachi, the plates." She pointed to the table then left the room.

Demetrius headed out of the house, and Malachi picked the empty dishes from the table. I helped him since Tylia hadn't given me any instructions. We stood in the kitchen, working in silence, until we heard the front door open.

"I guess it's time."

I looked over my shoulder as if I would be able to see through the walls.

"Okay, come on. Might as well get this over with." He grabbed my hand and lead me out of the kitchen, through the dining room, and into the living room at the front of the house.

I wished the house were bigger, just to prolong the introductions. In the room were four men, previously described to me as brothers, but they looked nothing alike. There was the short one called Eric. He had short light hair that matched the creamy tones of his skin and eyes; he seemed relaxed, yet anxious at the same time. A toothpick rested between his full lips, covered in bite marks.

There was the tall one with the huge afro and dark skin; Eric called him Shelly, but Malachi greeted him as Sheldon. His deep voice boomed through the house. When he smiled, I could understand his alpha status. His physical presence and obvious magnetic charm were a lot to take in.

Charles was also dark-skinned, but he was shorter than Sheldon and had a more muscular frame. His wired framed glasses and hearty laughter were comforting. I imagined he was the type

I could spend hours talking to and never tire of the conversation. I also pictured him spending hours in a gym to get the definition of his arms. He was the quiet one of the group; more reserved and observing of his brother's antics.

Jeremy was the last I saw. A slender frame but also toned. He had tawny skin and wore an enormous smile on his face as he looked at me. I was sure he was the only one who had noticed where I stood behind Malachi.

The other three greeted my escort with big hugs and hard pats on the shoulder, and just as I thought they would notice me, Demetrius entered the room, and they all greeted him instead. I shrugged it off and sat on the couch while the boys played catch up. There was no sense in taking it personally. It wasn't until about fifteen minutes of their ignoring me I finally said something.

"Okay, rude. You think you might want to introduce me at some point?" I poked Malachi in the back, but he didn't respond. "Seriously?"

"They can't hear or see you. Well, Jeremy can, but the others can't." Tylia rounded the corner. "Never been able to hide much from that boy. Good thing I trust him. Not that I currently have any other options."

"Wait, why are you hiding me?" I backed away from her and tripped onto the sofa. What reason could she have for doing this? I knew I didn't trust her! The woman was going to kill me with her so-called sons standing watch!

"Calm down, child. I just wanted to talk to you without having them boys all up in everything." She pointed at Malachi and Demetrius and shook her head slowly.

"What about Jeremy?" I nodded in his direction, afraid to take my eyes off the little woman.

"Well, for him, we will use the old fashion technique and simply leave the room. We couldn't do that with your protectors over there. They would never allow it, especially considering they're both bonded to you now. That's one tricky situation you got yourself into now, isn't it, honey?" She smiled and pointed to the back of the house. "Come on, let's chat."

CHAPTER 20

"Syrinada, I have been waiting** a long time for you to show up," Tylia announced as we walked through her home.

"You have?" I looked over my shoulder to the room where my protectors remained engaged in conversation.

"Yes, I have always known of you, your presence, but I never thought you would end up here or be so beautiful. They all seemed so determined not to let this happen. But you know, at the end of the day, what happens in the grand scheme really isn't up to us."

"No, I suppose it isn't," I agreed. If it were, I would still be in Chicago, headed to work, or hanging out with Latasha.

"I can understand why my boys are at each other over you," she spoke as she led me into the kitchen. "Hence, my choice to hide you until I could teach you a few things about being a siren that the boys can't. You know, like how to control that pull of yours. It's one of the strongest I have encountered, and you are still very young. I can only imagine the vixen you will be. Regardless of this, I can't have all six of my boys battling it out to get to you."

"My pull?"

"Yes, you're a strong young siren, and you, like the rest of us, emit a pull to the males of our species. Each siren does, but being that you are clearly an alpha that has that magical blood of your father flowing through your veins, well hell, even I am drawn to you, and Tylia doesn't swing that way, child." Her shoulders shook with her laughter. "So, you must learn to master it. Emit only what you desire and control your body's physical responses."

"Will this fix Malachi and Demetrius? Will it break their bond with me?" I asked, hopeful, though I had read of no such thing.

"No, unfortunately, that is something only you can do. Choose between the two of them." She stared at me. "Or choose neither. It doesn't seem to me as if you're really tied to either of them." I looked away, and she sucked her teeth. "Ah, well, that doesn't matter now, anyway. You're young. Plenty of time for all that puppy love, heartbreak, and such."

"Okay, so how do I do it?" I wanted to change the subject. I couldn't contemplate hurting either of them. And talking about it with the woman who was practically their mother felt wrong.

"To begin, you must become one with your own self. You must learn your body and its triggers, and identify the things that excite you, the things you desire above all others. Your responses to those triggers are what you need to regulate," she explained. "Yes, you will always get excited, but you must block that from emitting from you and spewing out into the physical world."

"How do I do that?"

"Think of being stoic and indifferent toward the opposite sex. If you can, imagine them as prey. You are an animal on the hunt, and your target only sees you when you are ready for them to. You must blend in with your surroundings, not stand out." She touched my hand, and I felt my flesh tingle.

"What was that?" I pulled my hand away from her.

"That is my pull. Can you feel it?" She touched me again, and I nodded. "Mine is gentle, kept tight to me, so that only the one

I want to feel it will. Let me show you how yours feels to those touched by it."

Tylia pulled up two chairs and sat them facing each other. She sat in one and pointed for me to take the other. After I sat down, she pulled my hand into hers and smiled.

"You ready?"

"Um, I'm not sure." I shook my head.

With a sly smile, she took a deep breath and looked me in the eye as she exhaled. The tingle ran up my arm and across my body. It purred as it spread and consumed me. I closed my eyes, trying to steady myself. When I opened my eyes again, Tylia was a different woman. She was alluring, far more beautiful, and intoxicating. I felt my body churning and responding to hers, and she quickly pulled her hands away from me.

"Whoa there, girl. That's what I'm talking about." Tylia put the top back on her pull and shook her finger in my face. "That desire you felt, contain that. Focus."

"Okay, that was weird and intense." I took a deep breath as my body tried to relax, and Tylia's appearance returned to normal.

"Yes, I know. Now it's your turn." Tylia held her hand out to me, an invitation for me to practice on her. "Dial it down. Center yourself. When you're ready, go for it."

"Okay." I reached out and touched her, and in a second, she was out of her chair and in my lap. She nuzzled my neck and purred like a kitten. "I think I did that wrong."

"Yes, very wrong." She purred again, and I could have sworn she was about to lick me. The thought of her tongue running across my skin completely turned me off, and she climbed down.

"Okay, what happened there?" she asked as she reclaimed her seat, completely unfazed by what had just happened.

"I don't know. I just had an... unfavorable image." The awkward smile stretched across my face.

"Good. Whatever it was, keep it, collect more, and store them in your brain. Keep those images on rotation, especially when you are around the men of our people. Trust me, women do not take kindly to young thangs showing up and turning their men's heads. I think that is true no matter the species." She melted back into her seat, fanning herself lightly with her hand.

"Okay, and if that doesn't work, what do you do?" I watched her closely, not sure whether her pull had fully released me yet or if mine was still holding her.

"To be honest, everyone has their own methods, and those methods change over time. Apparently, for you, the method is

to be disgusted. Thank you for that compliment by the way."
She peered at me.

"No, I didn't mean... I am so..." My face warmed with pooled blood.

"Child, stop!" She laughed. "I'm only poking at you. Okay, well, let's test this a bit before we unleash you." She smiled again, and then suddenly, her appearance changed.

Sitting across from me wasn't the sassy adoptive parent of my friends. Instead, Demetrius stared at me. First fully clothed and then without his shirt. His hand rested between his legs, patting the temptation between his thighs. And just like that, I was ready to go. I thought about all he could do to me and how I hadn't experienced it the last time, because Malachi interrupted us.

"No, stop, that is what I mean." Demetrius waved his hand and shifted from man to woman. Tylia looked disappointed. "You must remain focused and in control at all times."

"How did you do that?" I questioned Tylia who simply smiled and rolled her eyes.

"That is a lesson for another day and one that will take a lot of time; time you don't have right now. So, how about we try this again?" I couldn't resist or try to buy time; she had already shifted this time to Malachi and back to herself. "Whoa girl, rein it in!"

"I'm so sorry." The entire thing was an embarrassment. My arousal was instant and uncontrolled. I felt like a wild animal.

"Don't apologize, just focus." She softly smacked the back of my hand.

Over the next hour, Tylia tested my control. She shifted between forms, and not just the brothers, but also other random men I had never even seen before. Finally, I had gotten it under control, or at least to a level that seemed good enough to please Tylia. She said I would need more practice, and that I should be okay enough to be around her sons, but she still warned me she would intervene if necessary.

I swallowed the nervous lump in my throat as Tylia announced she was dropping the veil that hid me from the brothers. If what they experienced was anything like my reaction to Tylia when she ramped up her pull, this could very well be a total disaster. I understood that clearly for the first time. Hearing a description of something is nothing like experiencing it yourself. If that was what Malachi and Demetrius had to face day in and day out while being with me, I appreciated them so much more for not giving in.

"Focus," she whispered back to me just as we entered the room, and each man paused. Their heads whipped around toward me. I gulped and tried my best to squash the urges I could already feel rising. I thought of as many horrible images as I could, even the one of Tylia licking me, but it seemed impossible. Then, the image of the Sleeper slipped to the forefront of my mind, and there it was. The black snake dripping with slime gave me the control I needed. I took another deep breath and spoke.

"Hi, guys. You mind introducing me to your friends?" I looked at Demetrius, who blinked as if he had seen a ghost, and then parted his lips to make the proper introductions.

After the meet and greet was over, Tylia directed me to my bedroom, away from the guys. She gave me a high five and a, "You go, girl!" That little woman was seriously something strange. Not long after she left, was there a soft tapping on the door. I took a moment to center myself and focused on restraining my pull before I opened it.

"Hey," Malachi spoke. His familiar face and peaceful presence provided an instant sense of comfort.

"Oh, it's just you." I exhaled, releasing the breath from my chest, and accidentally, my pull.

The pulse slammed into him and bounced back at me. Before I could blink, he was on me. Malachi scooped me up off the floor and had me in his arms, carrying me across the room. He slammed me down onto the bed and ripped away my clothes and kissed my neck and breast. He growled as he rolled his hips, pressing his groin into me, and I felt him growing as he did.

"Sy," he spoke my name in a deep tone that had my insides burning for him.

I moaned and heard the door slam closed behind him, although neither of us had moved a muscle in that direction. Within moments, I was nude, and he was thrusting inside me. The air became heavy with the scent of sex, and it wasn't long before the banging began.

Pounding on the door that at first sounded like my own heartbeat, I used it as a guide for the rhythm of my hips as I flipped to change positions so I was on top of him. He reached up and released my hair from the bun, and it fell, covering my back, shoulders, and breasts. He pulled it all behind my neck, wrapped my hair around his fist, and pulled. My head fell back, and I let out a deep moan just as the door broke open. Splintered wood littered the room, and Demetrius charged the bed.

Malachi pushed me aside, and completely nude, went after his brother. Just as the men were about to clash, I heard Tylia yell for them to stop, and they did, just that simple, frozen in place. Their chests rose and fell heavily with aggravated breaths.

"Malachi, dress, please," Tylia spoke, and he did as commanded, absent-mindedly pulling on his clothing. "You too, Syrinada. I can't command you to listen to me, but I hope you will oblige my request."

I did as she asked, pulling a new shirt from my bag, then stood and watched as she whispered something into Demetrius' ear and slipped a chain around his neck. From it hung a small charm like Malachi's that glowed a soft orange before dimming; it was then that I noticed the changes in his appearance; he wasn't all man. He was just like his brother.

He was in transition, shifting to the beast that lay dormant inside of him, trapped by the charm he apparently had left behind. I shifted my eyes to Malachi, noticed that his charm still was in place, and realized that had Tylia not stopped them, Demetrius could have killed him.

Demetrius' eyes glazed over, and he left the room just moments before the same thing happened with Malachi.

"Well, that takes care of that." Tylia closed the door behind her, shook her head, and smiled. "Child, you are a handful."

CHAPTER 21

"I'm sorry. **I don't know** what else to say." I slumped down on the edge of the bed. "I don't know what happened. I just lost it, but that hasn't happened before. He has never..." I trailed off, not sure how to express myself to this woman who had raised the man I was just riding not moments ago on the same bed I was sitting on.

"There's nothing to be sorry about. I guess I should have warned you." She sat next to me, not at all concerned about what had just happened there. "It was one of those 'Oh shit!' moments. I realized my slip up just as it was happening. I never warned you about letting your guard down. The moment you relaxed, you released everything you held back. You do that slowly, like baking a cake. Easy does it, or the damn thing deflates, and everyone's mad."

"Oh." Well, that was good to know. Luckily, she was around to stop things. I couldn't imagine what would have happened if she hadn't been, or what Demetrius would have become. How long would it have taken me to notice? I wouldn't have been able to stop him or to save Malachi.

"Yeah." She looked at me and lifted my chin with her thin finger so she could see my eyes. "Are you okay, child?"

"I don't like this." I shook my head. "I hate that I've come between them. Demetrius could have just killed his own brother because of me. I don't want that." I couldn't stop the tears that shed at the idea of Malachi dying at the hands of his own brother.

"Yeah, I know, a dirty little love triangle. I have seen a few of them in my time, but you three take the cake. Three half-breeds. Damn shame." She shifted in her seat, obviously uncomfortable with the topic.

"Half breeds? I mean, I know their mom was kind of messed up when she had them, but does that classify them as half breeds?"

"No, her being out of her damn mind doesn't." She shook her head. "But the fact that their daddy was a demon sure as hell does."

"What?" My jaw fell open. Tylia used her hand to shut my mouth for me.

"I'll take that open fly trap to mean you didn't know about their father. Perhaps I should have checked to see if they had told you. I apologize." She paused and took a deep breath; yes, she knew I wanted details. "The boys' mother was horribly misguided, and much like your own, she fell in love with what some would say was the wrong guy."

"A demon." I thought I would choke on the taste of the word.

"Yea, he was a demon. They were happy together. When you're young and in love, that is all that matters. But that loved changed her. Together they thrived on hate and pain. As with most terrible pairings, someone took a stand against them. An angel, at least that's what everyone described him as. He came from nowhere, and in a flash killed them both. Before we had time to consider what had happened or who he was, he was gone. He gave them no chance to defend themselves, and he returned to the heavens, or wherever he was from."

"So, demons and angels." It just kept getting better.

"Isn't it interesting how much is real? Those angel-like beings have been in our history, stepping into conflicts and resolving them when we couldn't. It nearly came to that when we warred with the witches, but the world found balance on its own."

"So, Malachi and Demetrius are demons." I shook my head. "Demons?"

"Those two boys were the product of a romance fueled by hate, and somehow, they came out of it good and with pure hearts. I am not sure how that happened, but I know I don't want them to change." Her last words were more than a part of the story she told. It was her warning to me. The brothers meant the world to her, and she would do whatever she could to protect them, including taking action against a confused newbie siren.

"So, that's their actual forms? What Malachi showed me, it wasn't some mutation of birth, but how he really looks?" I didn't need to acknowledge her warning; we both knew the meaning behind her words.

"They have multiple authentic forms, just as you do. It's just both of yours are appealing to the eyes. Theirs, not so much. Those little charms they are wearing, they keep that ugliness from their daddy's side locked away." She patted me on the knee. "Get some rest, child. You will need it tomorrow. We go to see my good ol' friend Cecile. She sees all, and my gut tells me what she sees for you may not be pleasant."

Tylia got up from her seat, kissed me on my forehead, and swayed out of the room, humming. I climbed into the bed, assuming that after all that just happened, I wouldn't be able to sleep, but in a matter of seconds, I drifted to a comfortable state of unconsciousness.

You know that moment when you decided it was time to wake up? It was a nudge that pulled your brain from the grips of sleep and thrusted you back into reality. I had that moment. My dreams were pleasant, and my body felt rested, but something was different. Before I could open my eyes to process my surroundings, I had the distinct feeling of floating, like I was drifting on a current in the water. When I opened my eyes, I fucking panicked!

Light reflected from the glass, blinding me momentarily. I lifted my hands to shield my face and felt the water pushing against my skin. That was when I realized the floating feeling wasn't the remnants of a dream that refused to leave me. I was submerged in water, inside a fucking tank!

My first thought was that I was drowning, and I had to get out. I kicked my legs, pushing to the top. My heart stopped when I found a set of bars sealed me inside. I slapped the top. Panic consuming me, I swam around, trying to find an escape, but there was none. I returned to the top of the tank, wrapped my fingers around the bars and struggled to pull them free; I pressed my face between the bars, gasping for air. My cries for help went unanswered.

"Are you done?" Tylia's voice called out, and I searched for her.

Swimming to the edge of the tank, I saw her standing outside the structure.

"Get me out of here! What the hell is this?" I yelled at her. I knew that little woman was nuts! Was that her plan all along? Get me to drop my guard so she could trap and torture me?

"This is a crash course, honey; you're going to need to learn to be a siren, where it counts. Something is telling me there isn't time for a gentle push into the shallow end, so here we are." She smiled brightly.

"Look, I know how to swim, this is unnecessary." I tried again to move the bars that locked me inside the tank.

"Yeah, that's good. You know how to swim. I bet you haven't even taken a second to consider you were sleeping underwater.

Breathing, not swimming, you should be dead, right?" It was apparent that Tylia liked the direct method. No beating around the bush a siren shock therapy.

"I..." I stopped speaking because I realized she was right.

"This is the moment where you have this grand discovery of being a siren and go swimming off into the ocean with your pretty new tail!" She smiled at me and then laughed! "I had to do it, sorry, but you know this isn't going to be that simple, right?" She frowned at me.

"It never is!" I shook my head.

"Glad you've learned that lesson. Now, let's begin. Dive!" she ordered.

"What?"

"Go under the water, child." She pointed down.

I stared at her, expecting her to say something else. She didn't. Instead of further protest, and realizing that I wouldn't get out of the tank without doing what she said, I took a deep breath and dropped beneath the water.

"Stop holding your breath. It's unnecessary." Her lips did not move, but I heard her voice ricocheting through my mind.

I opened my mouth to ask how her voice got in my head and choked on the water. I pushed back to the surface and gasped for air.

"What the hell?"

"Get back down there."

"I—"

"Down!" she ordered.

I rolled my eyes and again dropped beneath the surface.

"Speak with your mind and your heart." She nudged, and I could feel what she meant. It was a deeper form of communication.

I focused on what I wanted to say and pushed those thoughts out to her. *"Tylia."*

"Simple enough, huh?" The smile stretched across her face.

I nodded my head in response, because simple or not, I was still unsure about this entire situation.

"Okay, breathe. I can see you trying to hold on to the air. If you do that, you will pass out. Relax your body and allow it to adapt. It will." I attempted to do what she suggested, unsuccessfully, and choked.

She didn't speak. She waited for me to swim to the top, collect myself, and try again. It took a few attempts for me to get it right. Whatever happened to the snap of a finger and all things being understood? That was how it went in most of the books and movies. The protagonist finds out they're special, and five minutes later, they understand everything about their new abilities. What a rip-off!

I guess that is where the saying *"practice makes perfect"* comes from. Yeah, right! The entire time as I struggled and reset, Tylia stood there and watched me. She wasn't pushy. Half the time she looked as if she had zoned out and her mind was in another world.

"Are you done?" she asked after she finally noticed I had normalized.

"Yes." I nodded, and she chuckled.

"Okay. Ready for the hard part?" She clapped her hands together, and again, that bright smile returned to her face.

"That wasn't the hard part?" I shook my head. *"Great!"*

"No, the pain you are about to feel, that is the hard part. You're going to shift, Syrinada. You will become your authentic form as a siren." Her words were slow, calm, and added emphasis and urgency to the matter.

"How do I do that?"

"Well, that is the best part about this crash course system I have here. You don't have to do anything, at least not the first time around. The first time, you only have to experience it, and later, you can more easily call that side of yourself forward." Tylia paced the floor, no longer looking at me.

"I've found that it actually creates something of a learning curve," she continued. *"Usually, it takes ages for a siren's first shift because of the fear they have of the pain and discomfort. Since we left the water, well, all things are more difficult. Those who were raised on land never knew the freedom of their tails. This way eliminates that hesitation. It won't take away the pain, but it will remove the mental block you don't even know is there."*

"Wait, I don't understand."

Tylia gave no further explanation. Instead, she smiled, and a moment later, a gray substance leaked into the water. The cloud moved quickly, coating my skin. I struggled against it, but there was no point. It covered me entirely before invading my body. Every opening was a passage for its intrusion. I fought as it seeped into my eyes, ears, mouth, and nose.

Against my will, my eyes slammed shut. Though I couldn't see Tylia, her thoughts still reached my mind. She urged me to relax, to let the substance do its job, but how could I? I felt like an alien was taking over me and she wanted me to just give in to it.

"Syrinada, you must let this work. The harder you fight it, the longer it will take, and the more pain you will feel."

"How am I supposed to relax? I can't. This isn't right."

"It's the only way you're going to learn this in time. Let go, child!"

I didn't like it, but I knew she was right. This wouldn't end just because I fought it. I'd already lost the battle. I cleared my mind of all thought, pushed away my thoughts of self-preservation, and thought of the only things that brought me peace. The framed picture of my mother. I brought her face to mind and hoped this experience would bring me closer to her.

It worked. My muscles relaxed, and the moment they did, the pain rammed into me. My body trembled, and my mind flooded with throbbing pulses of pure agony. Nothing existed outside of the pain. It consumed me, and I could do nothing to defend myself from the onslaught. I accepted it. My screams internalized. I allowed the alien to control me.

It lasted for so long my body felt like it would give out. Just as I thought I'd signed my own death certificate, it was over, and I opened my eyes again. I shifted through the water to see Tylia, now accompanied by my two protectors. All of them looked at me with faces of astonishment. Tylia smiled, nodded, and pointed behind me.

I turned around to see myself reflected in the side panel of the tank. I felt tears leave my eyes, only to become one with the water that held me. Nude body, my breasts floated freely above a bare stomach, and my navel rested just above scales.

Beautifully overlaid in multicolored patterns; apart, a rainbow of colors, but together, they blended to create a red hue with a spiral of gold that performed a synchronized dance as I moved in the water. Turning in circles, I admired myself. I couldn't help it, and I held my breath, regardless of the warnings of losing consciousness.

My hair moved around me, and even it seemed different, more alive. I touched my new bottom half, the part of me that wasn't there before. My tail was long and ended in a fiery point that looked like it was burning beneath the water, but I felt no pain.

In my head, I heard the admiring thoughts of Malachi and Demetrius. I looked for Tylia, but she was no longer there. I couldn't help but smile at Malachi. The tip of my tail swirled a bit as I did, and then I felt Demetrius' anger.

The small hand gently landed on my shoulder, and I turned to see Tylia, no longer with legs but a true siren. Her tail was gray with a dusting of green flecks that matched the green in her eyes. Instead of coming to a point like mine, her tail flare out at the end. It was what I expected a mermaid's tail to look like. I couldn't help but wonder what the others would look like with their tails. Perhaps the colors and shapes told a story about the person. A visual representation of their true selves.

"How do you feel?" she asked.

"I feel... good. No more pain." I smiled; happy the agony was over.

"Good. Now, I want you to swim. It's different from before." She nodded and performed a demonstration as she swam around the perimeter of the tank. She circled back and returned to me.

"Okay." I nodded, but I was unsure. Swimming was second nature to me. I had always loved the water, but this was different, and when I really considered it, the tail felt like it weighed a ton. How would I be able to move all of it?

Tylia placed her hand on my stomach. *"Breathe and focus. Your core is key. The tail adds speed, but the power comes from your center. Consider it like walking on land, not something to think about, you just do it. It's not a conscious decision; it's your body's normal function. The best way to approach this is to imagine getting out of a chair and walking across the room."*

"Okay, I will try."

For the first time, this lesson didn't take long. I took to it naturally, and in minutes, I was swimming confidently. There was more to learn, but Tylia felt confident that she had shown me enough of the basics she felt I needed to know. She then showed me how to shift back. A painful process that they all promised would get better with time.

Once my impromptu lesson was over, we climbed from the basement, where they stored the massive tank. Tylia fed us, gave me one hour to relax, and sent us off to meet the Seer. I found it hard to look at Tylia as we were leaving because I knew the smile that held residence in her features was a false front. Tylia knew we were walking into a shit storm; she just didn't possess the power to tell me exactly what it was.

CHAPTER 22

*"***W***hat is up with Tylia?"* I asked Malachi as we rode along in the back seat of the SUV. Neither of us wanted to be too close to his brother, a sentiment Demetrius shared. If he could extend the cabin of the vehicle, he would have.

"What do you mean?" He gave me a knowing side-glance and smiled.

"I mean all of that freaky, magic-like stuff she does. How is that possible? Is she like me?" I couldn't hide the hope that seeped into my tone.

It would have been a relief to know I wasn't the only outlawed person of coven decent, or that Tylia could show me a lot more about that side of my bloodline. For a moment, I had hope but Malachi's expression squashed that. His next words would disappoint.

"No, she isn't like you, Sy. I don't know of anyone who is. I'm sure it's not impossible." He shifted in his seat, turning so he could look me in the eye, when he continued. "Tylia was one of the sirens who fed from the human men. She just stopped before it completely corrupted her. She gained a lot of useful talents, which she kept. Some people said it changed her, made her more... energetic."

"Energetic, right." I sighed and looked out of the window. I hadn't realized just how alone I felt until then.

Once again, I felt the impact of denial as it slipped away from me. Yes, Malachi was different, but at least he had his brother to share those differences with him. I was alone, with no one to understand my internal conflict.

"Wait, she is one of the sirens that caused the war? How old is she?"

"Hell if I know." He chuckled. "Powerful sirens are basically immortal. Our lifespans vary based on a lot of factors like bloodline, and power level. But if you ever find out her true age, you let me know."

We arrived on the outskirts of Honey Island Swamp as the sun reached its peak in the sky. As they prepared the small boat that would carry us across the swampy waters, Malachi explained to me that the place was a tourist attraction, so we would have to take a more dangerous path to avoid being spotted.

Apparently, it was a hot spot because of the supposed Bigfoot sightings. He told me I would be safe if I did nothing foolish like stick my hand in the water. Yeah, that wouldn't be a problem. That was the last thing I wanted to be doing! My mind already convinced me that every floating log was an alligator.

As we floated along in awkward silence, with Demetrius once again at the wheel, I stared out at the beauty of the swamp. It was nothing like I imagined it would be. The place possessed an odd and inviting beauty. Large trees shot out and over us to rise into the sky. The limbs were teeming with life.

Beautiful birds and odd-looking bugs thrived where the branches touched down to skim the edges of the water. There were gators resting on fallen tree limbs who peered at us as we passed by, a reminder of Malachi's warning of not touching the water.

We passed a family of wild hogs who were near the edge of the swamp, herding their piglets together to keep them safe from the lurking alligators. Besides the odd smell of the water, the place was gorgeous and alluring with the oddities of nature, and

I could totally understand why someone would drive all the way across country to experience it.

"We're here," Demetrius announced and pulled the boat to a halt.

We were riding along on the boat for nearly an hour, and neither of them had said a word. The tension between them was unbearable, and the one time I thought about speaking up to say something about it, Demetrius shot me a look that told me I should back off, and I did.

"We're where?" I looked out ahead and saw nothing but more of the swamp and then shot him a sympathetic look. Was he so upset at how things went he was losing his mind?

"It's veiled to protect her," Demetrius said, as though it should have been so obvious.

He took out a small metal whistle and blew it. The small pitch bounced across the invisible wall in front of us, creating a ripple in the view. It shimmered and then dissolved. When the facade fell, it revealed a small hut. The structure was suspended in air, floating just above the surface of the water, fashioned completely out of the branches of the trees that surrounded it.

He slowly edged the boat up to the hanging steps and tied it down. I could see the gators floating beneath the house, eager to snap at our ankles as we climbed out. Malachi lifted me safely across and then did his own quick hop from the boat to the steps. Demetrius followed with his own little leap, but one of the snapping mouths nearly caught him. He kicked the gator, who threatened him with a low growl. He moved past us, grumbling as he took the lead.

A wall of hanging geraniums in a variety of colors covered the entrance to the hut. The flowers were the only thing about the place that didn't scream eerie swamp. They gave the place a soft scent that helped to kill the unpleasant swamp odor.

Across the threshold was a single room, and in the center of the floor sat a small woman highlighted only by the small beams of light that peeked through the cracks in the branches that formed her home. The woman had long, stringy, gray hair that hung down around her and spilled onto the floor like a rug extending from her head.

I frowned, trying to understand her attire. I'd expected the rings and string of beads that hung around her neck. It was the typical accessories of a psychic. What I didn't expect of a woman who dwelled in a hut that hung in the middle of a swamp was tie-dyed shirts and faded denim pants. When she looked up at us, she smiled with a wide yellow-toothed grin and eyes that were glazed over.

"Ah, you're here." She nodded at Demetrius.

"Yes, Cecile, thank you for seeing us on such short notice." He crossed the room and sat down to her left.

Malachi pulled me along and pointed to a spot directly across from the woman. I sat down where he indicated, and he took his place on her right.

"Anything for Demi." I could see this woman climbing onto him, much as Tylia had.

While she showed extreme affection to Demetrius, it was pretty clear she hadn't developed the same connection with Malachi, and she paid him just as little attention as she did me.

"This is Syrinada, and you remember my brother," Demetrius spoke without looking at either of us. This was going to get real old, and real fast!

"Aw yes, young Malachi, so much to see with you, your journey, oh how I love when you visit." Her statement made me smile because it erased some of my previous doubts about her liking him. Demetrius rolled his eyes, petty. "So, you're here because of the girl." She turned her glazed eyes to me, and my stomach clenched.

"Yes. We need to know how to protect her. I'm sure the covens are aware of her existence by now," Malachi explained. "They will make their move to strike soon enough."

"As well as the betrayals you have already uncovered, yes, this would create a conflict in the mind. Please relax so we can begin. Much to do today. I hate to rush you; you know how I love your visits, Demi." Once again, she focused on the older brother, and Malachi just smiled. I wished Demetrius could act the same when the tables were turned.

"Yes, I know." Demetrius nodded. "I will visit again."

"Ah." She shook her head. And I think I was the only one who caught the somber tone that resonated from her. Unspoken, she didn't believe that he would, or maybe she knew he wouldn't. "Well, let's begin."

With our circle on the floor already formed, she pulled out a small empty bowl and some colored stones.

"Your hand." She held her palm out to me.

I placed my hand in hers, and she positioned it just above the bowl and instructed me to leave it there.

"You two," she looked at the guys, "hush, okay? Let the magic work." She turned her glazed eyes back to me. "Syrinada, I need you to focus on the bowl and the stones. The bowl is the vessel, and the stones relay the story. Quiet your mind, and the spirits will confer."

I nodded, looked at both brothers, then closed my eyes. So many of these life-changing moments called for me to clear my head. The problem was, knowing so much depended on my ability to empty my mind made that a difficult thing to do. Still, I held my eyes closed and thought of peaceful things.

Everything slipped away. The smell of the hot water, the sounds of the critters outside, even the feeling of the men at my sides. It pulled away from me one by one until all was silent. Moments later, the silence was filled with the sound of moving water. The swamp danced beneath the hut.

I opened my eyes to see small funnels sprout up from between the floorboards and fill the bowl. The murky water swirled and lifted the stones, which danced in the current. I watched them closely and became hypnotized by their movement. When I looked up at Cecile, she was staring at me as if she were watching a movie. I was going to ask what she saw, but then the room filled with a fog that spilled into the center of our circle.

The ball of fog then flattened into a floating tablet. I kept my hand in place as I felt the thick fog rest on my skin. The sensation changed from a soft caress to tiny pricks and then to electric pulses like static charging. I felt one sharp sting, and I winced as it drew blood from me. The red liquid mixed with the gray smoke, and Cecile hummed. We all looked at her as she rolled her head in a small circle, taking deep, cleansing breaths.

"Syrinada, the spirits speak to me. There is so much coming for you, young girl. Dark things are happening, and your name is blended into the folds. Your aunt wields some ugly magic, and your father... your father is coming for you." She sat up straight, head no longer rolling, but eyes tightly closed. "You must protect yourself. There is a traitor in your midst, one who will bring you down. You must find your stone. You must protect yourself. The covens are aware. They fear your existence, and they are coming here. They will be here soon. You must leave soon, go now," she spoke calmly, her tone smooth like warm milk, soothing, even though her statement was one of urgency.

The fog dissolved and left my blood suspended in the air. I refused to move, afraid to disrupt whatever she was doing. Cecile opened her eyes and started a low chant. She reached out to Malachi and took a small knife from her pocket. With the blade, she made a small cut on his wrist. Slowly drops of his blood seeped from the opening, and instead of falling to the floor, they floated over to join the dance of my own. She did the same to Demetrius, and the blood from his veins moved to mingle with ours.

She reached into her other pocket, pulled out a thin coil, and held it out. The black metal unraveled and floated over to the blood mixture. She grabbed incense, lit it, and handed it to me, telling me it was okay to move my hand from above the bowl, which was now emptied of all its contents.

She continued her chant as I lowered my hand. The smoke from the incense circled the three of us before also moving into the mixture. It all pooled together and burst into a bright flame. When the flame died out, a small pendant of mixed breed blood wrapped inside of the coil floated in front of me. Cecile told me to grab it, and I did. I expected it to burn me, but it was cool to the touch.

I never spoke to Cecile. I held the pendant until she took it from me, attached it to a leather strap, and wrapped it around my wrist. The pendant hung flat against the back of my hand. I touched it and bit the inside of my lip. This was something special for protection, but it meant so much more to me. It was a part of them both, and no matter what happened, I would always have that.

She said her goodbyes to the boys, never to me. Once again, when she spoke to Demetrius, I got the feeling of her loss, even though he was still okay. I noticed how her touch lingered just a moment too long, and her head drooped as he walked away.

Driving back to Tylia's house, the brothers seemed to have shortly forgotten their hatred for each other and were busy making phone calls and a string of intricate arrangements for our departure. When we pulled up to the house, Tylia hopped into the car as they jumped out and told me to stay.

"I should help them." I reached for the door handle.

"No, you shouldn't. They won't be long. This is a pit stop. You must keep moving. I spoke to Cecile, and I know what is to come." She looked out the window at the group of men she called sons, though none of them were born to her. "Listen, I love those boys, and I know they must do what they are called to do. You need to allow it to happen. Allow them to do what they must. Whatever should come, do not stop them; do not stand in their way."

When she looked back at me, there were tears in her eyes begging to be shed, but she struggled to hold them captive. She would never let them fall... not in front of me, not now. She kissed me on the forehead and then the cheek and hugged me as tightly as she could before she left the car. At that moment, with her small arms wrapped around me, I felt it. The same thing I imagined Malachi and Demetrius felt when she climbed into their arms. It was love, pure and simple, and I never wanted it to end.

CHAPTER 23

Tylia's words and touch remained with me as we drove off, leaving the horror-masked house behind us. We were headed to Corpus Christi, Texas, which meant another eight-hour drive in awkward silence. Once they finished their strategic planning, it was back to unspoken hatred, and it was completely silent inside the vehicle, outside of the jazz music Demetrius insisted on playing.

Malachi put on headphones and stared out the window, so I pulled out my sketchpad. That was the first leg of our trip until we stopped in Beaumont for food and fuel. That was when the shit hit the fan.

Just as we were all returning to the car, Demetrius growled and dropped his bag as the predator I had witnessed in him earlier returned, and Malachi pushed me behind him, showing his own display of ferociousness. It was then I saw the two men step out of the shadows. They weren't large or physically imposing, but they had put both of my alpha protectors in defensive mode.

"We have to get out of here!" Malachi growled.

"Yeah, I got that." Demetrius made a dash for the car, dodging several balls of fire that formed out of thin air in front of the two men that targeted him.

"Sy, hide!" Malachi pushed me back and yelled.

"What?" There was nowhere for me to hide. Surrounding the gas station was nothing but the stretches of open fields.

"Your escape trick! Do it now and get to the car!" His eyes begged me to move, but I couldn't just leave him behind.

"What about you?" I asked.

"I got this." He urged me to comply. "Sy, listen to me, move!"

"Okay." I focused and knew I'd succeeded when the two men's eyes searched but couldn't locate me.

I watched them closely and moved to the car but stopped when I heard the twisted sound coming from Malachi. It was a mixture of my siren call and a werewolf's howl. Because they could no longer see me, they turned their attention to him and started directing the shots at their new target.

The SUV pulled up to me, with a bruised Demetrius behind the wheel and a hole in the back-passenger door that still burned. I jumped inside, and he sped off just as another ball of fire hit the back of the truck and caused it to lurch forward.

"What about..." I looked over my shoulder, trying to locate Malachi, but I could not see him. The two figures disappeared back into the shadows.

"I am not going to leave my brother behind!" Demetrius growled and cut me off.

He continued driving. The further we got from the gas station, the more anxious I became. Ten minutes later, we pulled off the road, and just as I was about to protest, Malachi emerged from the line of trees and jumped into the car. Not two words were said before we sped off.

Demetrius took out his cell, calling to notify people of what had happened. He wanted us to have coverage on the last of our journey. Malachi instructed me to keep my shield up. It was the only thing stopping them from tracking us.

It was an hour before Malachi could convince Demetrius to let him tend to the wounds he wanted us to believe weren't really affecting him. Even if he had somehow pulled the wool over his brother's eyes, I didn't believe him. I could smell him changing and decaying as time passed.

Malachi drove the final three hours to Corpus Christi Bay, which was where the entryway was. Demetrius stretched out across the back seat and made multiple calls to check on the progress of things. He wanted the guys responsible for the fireballs that left the SUV nearly destroyed to be found before they could report back. That was if they hadn't already done so.

Occasionally, I would look over my shoulder at him and find an expression that told me he knew exactly what was happening to him. He had little time left. Malachi was in complete denial and went on and on in a continuous ramble about how Demetrius would be okay if we made it to the Bay in time. The waters supposedly had healing properties. We only needed to get him into the current.

It was when Demetrius clocked out of the conversations that Malachi really hit the gas pedal. I held back my tears. I couldn't take it. The smell of death growing and mixing with the wave of anguish flowed from both brothers. I wanted to help them, but there was nothing. When Malachi looked at his brother, I saw the tears there. I didn't know what to say or do.

Had I bonded with Demetrius, I could easily help to heal him. The flow of power went both ways between mates. But I wasn't. There I sat, trapped in a car and forced to watch a man die, a man who was bonded to me, and a man that I should have been able to help.

I didn't think we would, but we made it to the Bay with Demetrius still hanging on to the last threads of life. Malachi hopped out of the car and lifted his brother from the back seat. He ran through the docks, which Demetrius' invisible team had cleared out hours prior to our arrival.

Malachi moved so quickly, I could barely keep up with him. I made it to his chosen dock just in time to watch him dive into the water with his brother in his arms. Again, I realized how useless I was. The wait was unbearable. Would they ever return to the surface?

I stood there with my hands covering my mouth as I waited for them to reappear. My stomach clutched, and my head spun. Demetrius was gone. And Malachi... what about Malachi? I ran to the end of the dock, prepared to dive in and search for my friend, but came to a halt just as his head broke the surface.

"Malachi!" I screamed, a giddy sound, until I realized he was alone. "But, Demetrius..." I scanned the water around Malachi, but there was no sign of his brother.

"I'm here," the soulful voice I hadn't realized I already missed so much bounced across the surface of the water. I found him floating up to break the surface just to the left of me.

"It worked!" I squealed. He smiled at my excitement, and I blushed.

"Yes, it did." Demetrius swam across the bay to his brother and wrapped his arms tightly around him. I thought he would lay a big kiss on him, but he didn't. Still, it warmed me to see the affection between them.

They were brothers, and they had their own kind of bond, one that I hoped transcended the one they both had with me, because according to Tylia, I had a choice to make. A choice that would shatter one of the bonds that tied the brothers to me. It might even break them both. At least they would have each other, regardless of what happened with me.

"So, are you coming or not?" Malachi asked after Demetrius released him.

"Oh, um…" I looked around. "What about our stuff?"

"Well, this wasn't exactly the plan, but we can't take any of it with us. Someone will get it." He brushed away the topic and my flimsy excuse.

"Oh. Right. Okay." I stalled as I searched for another reason not to join them. I wasn't sure if I was ready to change again, and I knew I wasn't ready yet to experience the pain of the change. Tylia was right about the fear of pain creating a block.

"Look, I know you're nervous about all of this, but we're here, and we won't let anything happen to you," Demetrius spoke calmly. "Trust us. Jump."

I took a deep breath and jumped. Once again, I had no other option, no other out. I dove into the water, and as usual, found myself to be unprepared for what happened. Only this time, I was grateful for the surprise. The water held more than healing properties. It was transforming.

Within seconds of touching the cool liquid, my body had shifted to reveal my red tail with the golden spiral. The shreds of my jeans floated across the surface. I looked down and was happy to see that my top was still intact. I swam around and enjoyed the feel of the current.

The training tank was nothing compared to swimming in the bay. The movement of the water against my tail felt thrilling. I could feel everything from the vibrations of the waves above to the life inside the bay stretching out into the ocean. It was an exotic feeling that aroused me. I danced through the weightless feeling for a long while, but eventually the urgency of our situation returned to my mind.

When I searched the water for the brothers, I first found Demetrius, a long, dark blue tail moved beneath toned abs and chest. His locs floated around him as he moved toward me with a smile on his face.

"You look amazing," he spoke to me and swam a tight circle around my frame. I reached out and ran my hand along the length of his tail as he passed; I could smell his arousal as it tainted the surrounding water. His tail was like Tylia's flaring out at the end.

"You look pretty awesome yourself. This is completely insane." I smiled at him as he stopped in front of me and pushed my floating hair from around my face.

"I always wished I could have that, that first moment of experiencing this, seeing all of it through fresh eyes." He touched my cheek. *"Born to this life, it's all so... normal to me."*

"It's pretty amazing." I leaned into his touch and heard the low moan from him, his appreciation of my affection.

How could I help myself? We'd nearly lost him, and it wasn't until I felt his touch on my cheek that I realized how much that would have devastated me. How could I stop myself from showing my concern for him or my happiness that he was okay?

"I bet." I heard Malachi's voice in the back of my mind and turned to see him.

I gasped internally, because to put it simply, he was gorgeous. Beneath the body I had become so familiar with rested a long red tail that had spikes of gold along the length of it. I looked down at my own and saw how much it complimented it. To anyone, we would look like a perfect match, color-coordination and all.

I swam over to him as though pulled by the current. My hand ran along his tail, the same as I did with Demetrius. But something was different. When I touched him, the feeling echoed back to me through my own tail. A heat radiated from him and ran up my arm. The small pulses I felt along my tail were like a chemical reaction. I smiled at him, knowing he felt it too.

"We should get moving," Demetrius spoke from behind us. We both blushed. Neither of us wanted him to be there to witness what was happening. I didn't know exactly why, but the moment felt private, intimate, not to be shared with anyone but us.

"Where are we going? You never actually told me that part." I posed the question when I noticed the tight set of Demetrius' jaw.

"We're going home. Your home to be exact. You need to find your stone and that is where your journey must begin." Demetrius swam to the mouth of the Bay, where the water spilled out into the Gulf of Mexico.

"How do we get there?"

Malachi moved to my side, and his tail rubbed against mine. I had to swallow the moan the feeling incited. Now was not the time, but damn, did that feel amazing!

"We must cross realms as you know; our home is not visible to the human world. To get there and to see it, you must cross the pathway." As Malachi gave his explanation, Demetrius dove to the floor of the bay, and with the speed of a bullet, he smacked the surface with his tail.

Where his tail hit, a crack spread and a small beam of light shot up that just barely reached the surface of the water. It was a hypnotic shade of green, and it warmed the water as it spread until it was wide enough for a compact car to pass through.

"You ready for this?" Malachi gripped my hand as Demetrius swam toward the gateway, not waiting for us.

"No." I told the truth and swallowed my fear.

"I didn't think you would be." He squeezed my hand, and I tightened my grip on his as we swam into the warm emerald light.

Enjoyed this book?

Please take a few moments to write a review. Like comments on social media posts, reviews help Authors in so many ways.

Honest reviews of my books help bring them to the attention of other readers.

If you've enjoyed this book, I would be very grateful if you could spend just five minutes leaving a review.

(Oh, and return to read an excerpt of

Siren's Test)

A DIVE INTO BOOK 2

Siren's Test

USA TODAY BESTSELLING AUTHOR
JESSICA CAGE

2

*A*fter how insane my life on land had become, there was nothing I wanted more than an escape. I wanted to be free of being a hybrid siren/witch that was currently being hunted by a coven of witches and other unknown beings. I wanted to run from the idea that my family was so fucked up, and that my own aunt was the reason my life had been thrown into complete chaos.

Even with my desire to flee my life, I couldn't help looking back as I swam into the light of the barrier between the human and siren worlds. Who knew what insanity waited for me on the other side?

Still, my red tail with the hypnotic gold spiral pushed me forward. The initial feeling was an intense warmth as the emerald rays of light tinted my arms and hands green. What followed was a tingle of electricity accompanied by the sound of sparks. I tried to find Malachi's face and hoped for eye contact to give me a sense of reassurance, but the light was too bright.

All I could do was squeeze his hand even tighter and hope he didn't let me go. The heat intensified for just a few moments longer before it cooled. The difference was undeniable once we crossed over the barrier. We came through the other side into an open mass of water that was as clear as the air I once walked through in the human realm, and even felt a cool breeze as it moved across the skin.

My body was lighter in this realm. I hadn't realized how much effort it took to push through the water before. Once we crossed over, I felt as though I was moving without even a thought about the action. It was just like Tylia described.

"This is awesome!" I spoke, and my mouth moved to emit the sound. "What the hell? I thought it was only mind-speak under water?" I looked to Malachi, who smiled.

"That rule only applies in the human realm. Here, the water is different; we are different. On this side of the barrier the water is like air. We breathe it, and it nourishes our bodies," Malachi spoke as he swam ahead. His tail brushed against my own and caused it to tremble.

"Well, that is pretty badass. At least now I don't have to worry about choking." I laughed and swam around a bit, enjoying the airy feeling of the water. I knew it was there, but I couldn't feel it. It was pure and didn't sit on the skin like the water we had just left.

Demetrius said something to Malachi that I didn't catch and then swam ahead. I watched him leave; the strength of his muscles as he moved on was fascinating. A strong solid man above a deep blue tail, which stood in contrast to the rich hues of his brother's.

He refused eye contact with me, and I wouldn't try to force any connection to happen. We would have time to talk things out once we arrived at wherever they had deemed safe for us to be. I still didn't know where that was, but there was clearly no turning back now.

I noted the surrounding beauty as well. The reef that filled the space below us was a rainbow of colors. The small ecosystem was teeming with life. I could hear them, and it was all so clear, the chatter of the animals that dwelled along its surface. They were all so happy, and the sound made me feel more relaxed and more confident in my decision to follow my leaders.

I should have known it wouldn't last. Moments later, Demetrius, brother of Malachi and my second protector, came hurrying over the reef, yelling to us *they* were coming and that we needed to take cover.

It was a total ambush. It seemed completely unreal, but the second we crossed that barrier, our enemy was alerted, and they quickly responded. I had exactly four seconds to relish in the beauty of this new world before they struck. At least thirty mermen attacked us, launching nets and spears.

Malachi and Demetrius fought them off for as long as they could, but there were just too many of them, and my defenders were weaponless. The only ammo we had was whatever we could scavenge. This equated to rocks, and eventually, the weapons we could snatch from our attackers.

I tried to help them, and I did for a while. I had just pulled a man off Demetrius' back when another man grabbed by my tail and flung me into the side of the reef. My head smacked the surface, and my vision blurred as my ears filled with the sound of the tiny inhabitants' screams.

The impact of my head against the hard surface left me confused. It took a while for the effect to wear off, but I could still make out what was happening around me. Malachi shouted with elation that help had arrived, and the men he referred to appeared over a reef and quickly worked against our opponents.

The youngest brother continued fighting. But I couldn't see or hear Demetrius. My vision cleared just in time to watch a spear pierce Demetrius' body, and his blood seep out into the water. I screamed out his name at the same moment Malachi rushed over to his dying brother.

He ripped the charm from his neck, and it looked as if he would use it to plug the hole in his brothers' belly, but a burly man punched Malachi in the side of his head. Malachi shook

ABOUT THE AUTHOR

Jessica Cage is an International Award Winning, and USA Today Best-Selling Author. Born and raised in Chicago, IL, writing has always been a passion for her. She dabbles in artistic
creations of all sorts, but it's the pen that her hand itches to hold.
Jessica took a risk and unleashed the plethora of characters and
their crazy adventurous worlds that had previously existed only
in her mind into the realm of readers. She did this with hopes
to inspire not only her son but herself. Inviting the world to
tag along on her journey to become the writer she has always
wanted to be. She hopes to continue writing and bringing her
signature Caged Fantasies to readers everywhere.

Don't forget to sign up for the Caged Fantasies Newsletter!

Made in the USA
Columbia, SC
06 October 2023